Misdemeanor

TANYA MARIE LEWIS

Sadorian
PUBLICATIONS

Published by Sadorian Publications, LLC

Cover Design: John Riddick, Jr.

© 2002 by Tanya Marie Lewis

Library of Congress Card Catalogue Number: to be assigned
ISBN 0-9718148-6-4 (pbk)

First Edition
First Printing, June 2003
10 9 8 7 6 5 4 3 2 1

Published and printed in the United States of America

www.Sadorian.com

Acknowledgments

Glory and honor first goes to my Father in Heaven and my Savoir, Jesus Christ.

Dedication

To all the men and women, young and old, who left behind "conditional" love and entered into the fullness of an unselfish, unwavering, unconditional love that cannot be uprooted by man.

To My Late Grandparents

Willie and Mary E. Davis
And
Claiborne and Alice Lewis, Sr.

-Real Love, Real Marriages that continue in Heaven.

Psalm 127:1
Unless the Lord builds this house,
They labor in vain who build it.

Misdemeanor

PART I
To be yourself and accepted is love manifested into reality.
-Tanya Marie Lewis

The Crew and Me, The Crew and I
1983

Daddy's not coming home again. Before I heard those words we were the fabulous four from Ft. Knoxville, Mississippi. That's what Daddy use to call us. Now, we just three, not fabulous three-just three. Momma, my older brother, Mitch and me or is it, Mitch and I? Daddy would know and correct me, but he's not coming home again. I'm Malena, just turned eight yesterday so I don't know a whole bunch of stuff yet. Except them telling me today...Daddy's not coming home again. He called me Princess. Momma calls me hardheaded and Mitch just call me whatever he want when Momma not around. I thought Daddy moved to another house with three other people. Mitch just a year older than me, so he don't know where Daddy is either. Momma was crying too much to tell us anything else. She cried, so we cried too, even though we still didn't know where he was. We didn't have grandparents we could ask. Daddy said they all went to glory before me and Mitch, Mitch and I, was even thought about. We just have old Mrs. Mable from down the road. She told us we could call her grandma if we wanted to. But, she just Mrs.

Mable cause' she ain't went to glory yet.

Mrs. Mable used some small words when she talked about Daddy. Died. Dead. Death.

I wasn't fully sure what they meant, but I knew it wasn't good when all Daddy's friends and some folks I didn't know showed up at our house. Most folks was crying like Momma. I didn't know our little house could hold so many people. Probably why a lot of them went outside to sit, smoke and laugh. Seemed you had to go outside to laugh, cause' crying was left for inside. Me and Mitch, Mitch and I, still don't know what's going on. Old folks just keep hugging us saying, "they sorry to hear bout our Daddy." Said he was a good man. I started to cry because I didn't like what I was feeling. Where was my Daddy? I miss him right now this minute and he needs to come home. My Daddy be tall and dark, like the color of ripe blackberries but smooth like my new patent leather shoes. He got little dimples on the side of his face that make his smile seem bigger than it is and pretty dark eyes like Bambi. They say I look just like him, except I got Momma's skin color. She the color of the flaky skin on an onion-y'all know what I'm talking bout? And Mitch, look just like Daddy, skin color and everythang-he got the dimples too. I guess Daddy couldn't give them to both of us and Mitch was first in line, so I didn't mind that so much. I was sitting there thinking about that when I overheard Mrs. Mable saying, "death came knocking too early for Mitchell, po' man just thirty-three years old." I feel really bad now. I must have been sleeping something-hard 'cause I didn't hear a knock. I don't know about Mitch, but I would have made sure not to let death in, that way Daddy would still be here. He would be here to put these people out because I'm getting sleepy and Daddy wouldn't let us be up this late. I'm mad at Momma now-she must have opened the door for death cause me and Mitch, Mitch and I, wasn't allowed to answer the door. That's probably why she crying like she is. Serves her right.

Them next couple of days didn't get no better. More folks, more food, more confusion and I still don't know anymore about this death thing than I did before.

Momma woke me up on the fourth day, said I had to get dressed so I could go say bye to Daddy. I was happy. He wasn't coming home but she was taking me to see him. She said Daddy was at the church house, which was no surprise. Daddy loved church and always read to us from his tote Bible. I asked Momma if I could take Daddy's tote Bible with me. That's what he called it, his "tote" Bible.

Every time we went somewhere he'd say, "wait, let me get my Bible." I asked him one time why he like his Bible so much. He just said, "Princess, I tote this thing everywhere-its my protection." I guess Daddy didn't have his tote Bible the day he left cause it was in his room on the night table. Momma let me carry it cause she said that would make Daddy smile.

When we got to the church house, all the people who was at our house was waiting for us. Pastor Simms was there; he one of Daddy's friends too. In church, Momma sat between me and Mitch, Mitch and I, on the front pew. I kept looking around for Daddy but I didn't see him. And I'm starting to wonder what's in that big box with the flowers on top sitting in front of us. All of a sudden, Pastor Simms started preaching and it ain't even Sunday. He was talking bout Daddy so I listened. He kept saying my Daddy was a fruitful man, a small man in size but big in heart. My Daddy was a big man to me, the way he picked me up like nothing. Swinging me around in the air so my ponytails could fly with the birds. But he did have a big heart, so I didn't say nothing to Pastor Simms bout it then. I'm getting scared now cause' Mitch crying, act like he done figured out what this death stuff all about. Momma must have give her tears to Mitch cause she ain't crying, just looking at that box. She look pretty, she look sad and she wearing that black dress Daddy like on her so much. That would make sense, she here to see him too.

I looked around and he still ain't showed up. That wasn't like Daddy to be late for nothing. He made sure we were on time for everything. Pastor Simms was still preaching saying we'd see Daddy again some day soon and talked some more about all his fruit. I can't recall Daddy eating a lot of fruit, but Pastor Simms sound sure that he had some. I'll just look for it when I get home and put it up for him case he need it when he get back. The more Pastor preach, the more folks cry. So, I busied myself looking through Daddy's tote Bible while I listened. He had some dried brown roses in there, didn't know what they for-just looked at em'. Then Pastor introduce some lady who come from town to sing. She must have come to make folks scream, cause' that's what they did. I ain't never heard this much racket in the church house before and it got worse when the man from funeral party who was at the house the other day walked over to that big box. I couldn't wait to see what was inside. It must be a present for Daddy since we all here waiting on him and it ain't even his birthday.

The funeral party man opened the lid on that box and my eyes hurt at what I saw. My Daddy was in that box. Momma let out a scream from somewhere. I say somewhere cause it didn't sound like her. Sound like a hundred people screamed, "Oh Jesus," through her tiny body at one time. Folks started screaming and crying even louder than they did at our house. I didn't, I couldn't move and neither did my Daddy. It looked like him, but I say it ain't. Daddy always happy to see us; hugging and kissing us, but he just laying there now. That ain't my Daddy in that box. Not my Daddy. Last time I saw him was the morning before he didn't come home again. He came in my room before work like always. He hugged me real tight (tighter than most times) and kissed my forehead. He told me to be good and I said I would. That's what I'm doing now, being good for Daddy. I'm not going to cry like these grown folks. Maybe if I sit here being good, Daddy will get up out that box and hug me again. But he didn't. Aunt Caroline, Momma's older sister who come down from Chicago to say bye to Daddy took me and Mitch, Mitch and I, up to the box. Mitch just cried and said, "Daddy, don't leave us. Please Daddy, get up, wake up Daddy." I don't ever remember my brother crying bout nothing unless he was getting a spankin', but he was crying something awful now. I didn't cry though. I was being a good girl. Looking at my BIG Daddy in that LITTLE box with his eyes closed shut and a smile on his mouth. I smiled back at him cause he must have been smiling bout me having his tote Bible just like Momma said he would. After that they closed my Daddy back in that box and we all went outside where they put it in the dirt. Folks cried some more and help push the box down with flowers. The more flowers they threw the lower it went.

I waved bye to Daddy until I couldn't see his box no more. This death thing too much for my little mind to understand. But, I'm not sad. Pastor Simms said we'd see Daddy again so I'll wait. And I'll hold onto his tote Bible until then.

Any Day Now

About five days after Daddy left Mitch asked "You think these people will ever leave?"

"I don't reckon so-don't seem like it huh?"

"Stop talking like that Malena. Remember what Daddy told you about trying to sound like old people."

"I can talk anyway I want."

Anyway, these folks ain't bothering me too much; Mrs. Mable keeps bringing her special pecan and potato pies to the house. I'm like Daddy, just love Mrs. Mable's pies.

That's all we was doing now is eating, wasn't nothing else to do in the country. Mitch and I (I remember Daddy saying it's "I" not "me") went back to school two days ago, but now we just sitting here throwing rocks at the water pond in front of our house. Mitch real quite now, me too really. We come outside when they start talking bout Daddy and looking at picture books. Most of the stories we heard already. Daddy told us. He was always telling us his stories. He grew up a farm boy in this little town we live in now, raised by my grandparents in glory. They sent him off to fight with the civil rights movement people (still don't know them, but some of em' inside now) most times, that's what he done with his life. That's how he met our Momma. Daddy and his friends were in Chicago, say he went in a miller, no, millie, no militant, yeah that's it and came out married to the lovely, Sandra Wilkes. That's what Daddy always called her, the lovely Sandra Wilkes, like she was one of them colored folks on the picture tube we have.

Momma was in college when they met, studying clothes with a minor in movies. It's another name for it, but I just can't recall right now. But anyway, she left and never looked back they say. She must have been putting her movie skills to work lately, cause she was playing somebody other than our Momma.

Daddy's friends use to tease him bout Momma, specially, Uncle Will,(not my real uncle, daddy only chile), said, "boy where you going with that high and mighty woman you got…that's too much city woman for you." Daddy just grinned and said he had it covered. He must have cause they (those people inside) said Daddy made her country, too. She didn't seem to mind though. Every now and again, Momma voice change to something soft and high and she tell Daddy he bout as country as a row of collard greens. Daddy would just laugh and press his dark skin into hers for a kiss and a pat in a place he didn't think we knew about. Then they just looked at each other for the rest of the night, but in the morning she still country. She been country since I know her. They say it's a city somewhere, Daddy was supposed to take us to one, but we ain't been yet. He and Momma use to talk about moving to the city so Mitch and I could have a better life. Life was good in the country, so I can't wait to see what the city gone be like. I guess that's where Momma's spirit went. I heard Mrs. Mable telling Aunt Caroline, she was worried bout Momma. "Sandra's spirit don' dipped and went into depression Caroline. If it waddin' for dem youngins' she wouldn't be here," Mrs. Mable said. Aunt Caroline just nodded and cried some. Mitch said depression was the name of the city Daddy was gone bring us too. I know Mitch older than me, but that didn't sound right. I told him so too. He told me to be quiet that Daddy told him to take care of us.

"Stop lying Mitch, when Daddy tell you that?"

He stood up and threw a rock at me.

"I'm tellin Momma," I yelled.

"So, go tell you ole cry baby. I'm just telling you what Daddy said and you calling me a liar. Apologize Malena."

I didn't want to, but I did. Mitch was the only friend I had now, so no need in me getting him all fussed up and stuff. He say Daddy told him the morning he left home. I got excited, wanted to hear what else Daddy said.

"That's all he said Malena. Stop asking so many questions. He just said to take care of you and Momma."

I don't know about you, but sound like Daddy knew he wasn't coming back home. I just don't know what's going on anymore. I still haven't found Daddy's fruit Pastor told us about and now I gotta look for Momma's spirit, on top of letting Mitch take care of me. I don't know a whole bunch like I said before, but I know a grown man's shoes ain't meant for little boys. This just too many things for my young mind. Too much!

I bet Daddy didn't know he'd cause all these problems when he decided to stay away. He didn't like confusion. That was the only thing he say he didn't like-confusion. But he hated three things; injustice, violence and canned sardines and not necessarily in that order. I didn't know what injustice and violence meant. Well, sort of, cause' the stories he told us. But I knew what a sardine was and liked them. I asked Daddy why he hated sardines.

"Sardines make me sad Princess."

"Why they make you sad Daddy," I asked, while sitting on his lap one day.

"Cause you should never take a baby away from its parent-even if it's just a fish." I know it meant more than that and I'll understand one day, but for now I just won't eat those sardines that made my Daddy sad.

I forgot what I was saying. Oh, Daddy didn't know this would happen. He liked to make us laugh-all of us. He was always telling jokes, the only time he was serious when he was reading from the tote Bible, even when I asked questions-he stay serious. I remember when I was younger, around four I think, I asked,"Daddy, where God come from?"

He just smile real bright and say, "God is the beginning

Princess and the end, so He always been here."

"Always?" I couldn't believe somebody had been here always.

Daddy just laugh a bit and say, "Yeah, always, God knew all about you before u's born, even know how many strands of hair you got on your head."

I put my hands on my head and whispered. "God knows *alllll* these number of hairs?"

Daddy just laughed at me like I told him a large joke and picked me up and hugged me. "Yes, Princess, God knows everything."

I knew then God was big, cause even I don't know how many hairs on my head and its my head. So, I just always look up to the sky to see what else God know bout me sometimes while Daddy reading and being serious. But after tote Bible lessons he laughing and telling jokes. He didn't tell us all his jokes though. Cause' I know some jokes he told Momma wasn't meant for us. A lot of times he'd walk up behind her and whisper a joke in her ear and Momma light beige skin would turn plum red. I hated those whisper jokes, cause' every time he told her one, Mitch and I had to go to bed early. And Daddy told her ALOT of whisper jokes. They must laugh all night too cause' come morning they still grinning bout the joke from the night before. Yeah, that was my Daddy and he should be home any day now.

Crickets and Sunshine

School is out. I'm happy bout that. I like the summer time and the fresh air and the fat plums that grow on the tree in the backfield. We doing okay, I think. Mitch talking again and helping me read the tote Bible sometimes. I finally stopped waiting on Daddy to come back. I still miss him though. But I see now that soon means later in grown folks terms. I don't know why old people put sugar on sour stuff, but they do. They finally tell us a log fell on Daddy at the mill he worked for. My daddy was big, but he not big enough to stop a log from falling, God maybe, but not Daddy. If I knew that then I would have known it would take him longer to get home. Oh well, no matter. Mitch protecting me-keeping his promise to Daddy. Ain't much he can do bout Momma right now. She look different-real different and old like Mrs. Mable. All her clothes about to fall off her and she play with her food most times. That kinda makes me mad because we get a whippin' when we do it. Sides that, she taking good care of us like before. She still smile, just look at us more and don't hardly let us out the house except for when school in. She don't pay attention like she should though because she burn my scalp every Saturday morning with the hot comb.

21

She say, "Momma sorry baby, I wasn't paying attention." That's how I know she don't pay attention no more (I wasn't trying to be smart. Daddy made sure we knew our place as children). But how can she pay attention now? Her spirit went to the city, remember? But I'm looking out for her. At night I sleep for a bit, get up when I hear the crickets outside and sit by the window. Sometimes the windowpane catch my forehead when I doze off, but I stay up for the most part. I just sit there looking with my Daddy's eyes all night till the sunshine come up. I gotta make sure that death don't break in or knock at our door no more and take Momma too.

Please God!

I decided it was time to ask God for a favor. Daddy say that God give it to me, so I want to know if I can have it now. Momma's not doing good at all. Just seems she get up and go to bed. All of this because Daddy's not here. So instead of my watch tonight, I'm going outside to look at the sky to talk to God.

I could barely see walking through our dark living room. I was feeling my way around the furniture when something felt like a knife went through my foot. I screamed into my hand so I wouldn't wake up Momma. It's just Mitch's G.I. Joe toy. I can't even tell on him, (like I like to do) because Momma gone want to know what I'm doing up. Then my hand have to catch another scream, because it's a head on the wall with long ears. My little heart beating crazy until I realize it just the pom pom ball Momma got on the top of my head tied with ribbons.

I finally make it out the house and take my blanket and pillow and make my way to the back barn. That's where Daddy used to go when he said he needed time alone with God. So, I figure this must be the meeting place. It's after ten o'clock but it's not dark. God must have known I was coming because he turned on some extra stars so I can see. I spread my blanket out on the grass and put my pillow down so I can kneel on it. Momma and Daddy make us get on our knees and bow our head, something about humming ourselves before God. So, here I am now humming, but it don't feel right. Seem I should let God see my face so He know who I am. So, I flip over and lay on my back with my head on the pillow. This feels better, cause' I can see the sky and I know God up there somewhere.

So I say, "Hi God." Then I wave at Him, "Daddy say you his friend and I was wondering if I could be your friend too. I need a favor God. I was wondering if you would be my Momma's friend, too? She don't have any since Daddy left you know? I worry bout her God because she wear her hair real crazy now and don't hardly take a wash off or nothing. And I know she been playing with our color markers, because she draw black marks under her eyes now. So see, that's why I know she needs a friend God. I don't know how much you can do, but I promise to be good if you help her. I think if you show me where her spirit is, I can give it back to her and that may make her smile again. That's it God. And, oh, can you make Mitch stop picking on me all the time, that may help too-so Momma won't have to yell at him like she does."

After that I just lay there, waiting to see if God gone do me this favor. God didn't say nothing(Daddy say he'll talk to you) so I fell asleep until I heard that voice. Don't know where it came from, but it was low and loud. The voice said, "Daughter of Mine, go forth."

I raised up and looked around and didn't see nothing. I got scared then and started walking back towards the house. I was walking slow and that voice said it again, "Daughter of mine, go forth." I took off running so fast my ribbons slapped me in the face. When I got in my bed, I pulled my knees up to my chin and sat there thinking that voice was gone follow me inside. I know one thing, I'm not going back out to the barn again by myself.

Daddy Came Home
and We Moving

I was playing with my paper dolls three days later when Mitch come running in my room. He was out of breath real bad. I thought the boy was in trouble again. Mitch liked whippins', he had too because he was always doing things to get one. I was ready to give him one too when he knocked my doll to the floor. He was talking real fast, but my eyes got big cause I think I just hear him say Daddy home.

"What you say Mitch?"

He whispered, "Daddy's home Malena, he here right now in there with Momma."

I was scared, wanted to see him, but first thing come to my mind was how he got out that box in the ground. I never did say this death thing had began to make sense, cause it didn't. Then I started thinking God was giving me that favor I asked for the other night.

Mitch pulled me behind him to Momma's room and we pressed our ear to the door.

"I don't hear nuthin'," I said.

"Shhhhh!"

Right round that time, I heard Momma talking to Daddy. Sound like she was mad too, cause' she was yelling in capital letters. Then it got silent again, Daddy must have been whispering when he talked. I sure didn't hear him, but I knew when he was finished because Momma started yelling again. It wasn't hard to hear what she was saying, but it was hard to hear what she said. Make sense?

She told Daddy, "Mitchell, why you leave me with these kids by myself? What am I supposed to do with two mouths to feed? You lied, you said you'd never leave me and I believed you like a dummy."

Momma stopped yelling and started crying from her stomach. That made me cry for the first time since he left. I thought Mitch was gone tell me to shut up, but he put his arm round me and held me tight. Daddy would be proud of him if he came out the room to see it. We stood there a long time listening. Momma talked to Daddy some more, told him she wanted to be with him, then asked the Lord to take her to him. Mitch crying with me now, seems Daddy left and Momma don't want to stay with us, so it's just me and Mitch, Mitch and I now. He walked me back to my room and slept on the floor by my bed that night to protect me.

We could hear Momma crying and screaming at Daddy all night long to come get her. And I cried in my dreams not knowing if I'd have a Momma when I woke up in the morning.

Come morning Momma was smiling. Daddy must have told her something she wanted to hear in silence. She cooked us a big breakfast; slab bacon, grits, red eyed gravy and homemade biscuits and Mrs. Mable's homemade syrup. She ain't cooked like that since he left. He must have given her some money last night too cause while we were eating she say we moving.

"MOVING WHERE?" Mitch yelled.

That boy must have really thought he was the man of the

house for a second, till Momma sliced her eye at him.

"We're moving to the city, that's what your Daddy wanted."

That's when I noticed Momma's skin didn't look like pancake dough anymore, it had color to it and she didn't sound country either. Daddy must have gave her money and her spirit back last night cause she look free somehow. I was happy to see that, Mitch still looked upset, still Momma said we were moving by some water and a beach. I ain't never been to the beach before. Heard about one from one of Daddy's stories.

"Where the beach we going to Momma?" I asked.

I was ready to go pack my clothes right then because I remember how pretty Daddy said the beaches were.

"We moving to a place called Biloxi. Its still in Mississipi, it's about eight hours from here. It's kind of like the city and country combined, but there's more opportunities for us there."

Sound good to me so far.

"And, guess what, your Aunt Caroline's driving down to stay with us until we get settled."

I was real happy then, I loved me some Aunt Caroline. She wore real pretty clothes, not like I see folks in round here and she talk in that sweet, high voice like Momma using again. Almost sound like syrup hitting those biscuits we just ate. Smooth. Slow. Tasteful.

Daddy use to say they dainty women. I don't know what dainty mean, but Momma use to be dainty like Aunt Caroline- and sided to go back to it I guess. Aunt Caroline like another Momma, she has her own beauty parlor in Chicago. Fact, she combed my hair in ringlets the day of Daddy's funeral party. And I know when she come to help us move she gone bring me and Mitch. Oops, Mitch and I some presents like she always does. Momma said she had to tie up some loose ends with the house and then we were heading to our new life. She wanted us to get settled before school started in the fall.

Sure enough, a few weeks later Aunt Caroline drove down from Chicago in her brand new Ford Thunderbird. I had never seen a new car and the blue on it shined like the sky. Mrs.

Mable come down with plenty of food for us to take on the road trip. She cried like a young girl and said, "I don't reckon' I's be seeing you chilren' no mo," and gave us big hugs. I cried too. I was sure gone miss Mrs. Mable, she had stories too, no husband or children-just stories. Daddy say Mrs. Mable was rough in her old days, but time and the Lord mellowed her out.

She stopped crying long enough to tell Mitch to be good and grow up and make his Daddy proud. She looked at me real strange and hugged me real tight and said, "Baby, yo' Daddy showed you what God look like in a man, don't settle for anything less than God's best, ya hear me?"

I cried in her stomach and shook my head like I knew what she mean, but I don't. She talked with Momma some and then put our food wrapped in foil in the back window and we left and went to say bye again to Daddy.

Momma, Aunt Caroline and Mitch walked over where his box lay under the ground. I sat on my knees in the backseat with my hands pressed against the window looking out at them. I didn't want to say bye again, in fact I hadn't and didn't plan to. After that we left heading to the Biloxi place. Mitch and I played tic tac toe in the back seat for awhile, but the highway became too long for us and we feel asleep. We left fo' day and it was dark when we pulled in, Aunt Caroline got lost and we lost almost three hours. I was sleep, but I remember Momma waking us up, saying we were in the city.

God sent His Angel again

I didn't think I was going to like this Biloxi place. First two nights I didn't sleep. It wasn't like me keeping watch at home, cause this time I was trying to go to sleep. But after the third night I was okay because the angel came back in my dreams. You probably don't believe me, Momma and Mitch didn't either. Daddy was the only one who believed me. But when I was little, around four this angel started reading scripture to me from the tote Bible in my dreams. I knew it was from the tote Bible because Daddy read us the same things some time. And I couldn't read at four. Shoot, I can't read the tote Bible that well now. I can't see the angel though, just know he there. Don't know if it's a he really, just a voice. Soothing voice, just read and read and read some more. Then the voice say, "Daughter of mine, go forth." I don't know where I'm supposed to go, just know I sleep real good on the nights the angel come. Like I did last night. The angel must have known I was scared in this new place way from Mrs. Mable and my friends. I'm not going to tell Momma about it though.

She and Daddy got into a big fight when I told her the first time it happened.

She say, "Baby, you ain't heard or seen no angel, go sit

down."

Daddy say, "Don't say that Sandra. If she says it's an angel in her dreams it probably is. Children see things through the eyes of God and you let her see this world through His eyes as long she can. Cause' she gone see it through this worlds soon enough."

Daddy sounded like he was mad at Momma when he told her that. Like he knew something she didn't.

Momma didn't say nothing back to him though, just seemed like she looked at things different after that.

So, whenever the angel came in my dream, I'd tell Daddy. He'd ask if I could remember a verse or something the angel read to me. I'd tell him and Daddy would go right to it in his tote Bible and read to me again. Same thing the angel was reading. I'm telling you, God sends an angel in my dreams that read from the tote Bible. You believe me don't you?

No Sugar No Salt

Biloxi didn't roll out the red carpet when we came to town. But somewhere between hot combs and cornrows things began to turn around for us. The first year was hard. Momma found work cleaning at a hotel but it didn't pay much. She didn't seem to mind though. She just said, "God knows our needs and He will provide," she lived on that principle. God was sure faithful to us. I watched Momma many nights take fifty dollars, pay something on all the bills and still had money left for food. She is a WOMAN, you hear me? At least that what Daddy would say if he were here to see her. Momma never has pity mission parties for herself either. She said, "I'm too busy to be sad, I got a blessing I'm trying to catch up with." That second year I think she was ready to let go of the pain because she took Daddy's photos down and stop reading all those love letters he wrote her. I'm still young, but Mitch and I knew she still loved him. But her life wasn't in the past anymore, she said. "Until the day I die, no one can take your Father's memories. If the pictures burn-he's still in my heart. If his letters burn-he's still in my heart. I love you kids, but I want you to have a better life, a more abundant life and I can't give that to you if I try to force yourself to stay in a place I'm not supposed to be."

A few days after she told us that we were out shopping, well, looking. We didn't have money so Momma was sewing most of our clothes, but you couldn't tell. It was fashion design school she went to. I think I said clothing school before, but what can you expect I was eight when I told you that. I'm older now, turned ten last month. Well, we were in this fancy boutique in the Vieux Marche Mall. Just looking. This white lady, found out later her name was Mrs. Joan came out of the dressing room. She must have been looking around for a sales clerk-couldn't find one, so Momma had to make do.

"Excuse me, but how does this dress look on me?"

She was very nice, some white people had been rude, but that was something else Momma taught us, every day is different and so are people. If its raining-stay inside. If the sun shining-go outside and enjoy it. She taught us many things, picked up where Daddy left off. And she was about to teach us about lying.

"Well," she said, "The dress is too tight and the color is all wrong for you."

Just like that-she didn't chase it with sugar, but she didn't use salt either.

Mrs. Joan didn't seem so friendly after that.

"Excuse me, who do you think you're talking to?"

Momma looked around, back at her.

"I guess I'm talking to you, since you approached me."

Mrs. Joan was about to say something smart and caught a glimpse of herself in the mirror. She must have realized Momma was right about that dress. And, God must have been watching out that day, because Momma helped Mrs. Joan pick out three outfits in the right size and colors. That's how it started for her. Momma calls it a miracle and I guess it is. That day Mrs. Joan who happened to be a true "Southern Belle" with the money to prove it, offered Momma a job as her personal shopper. Mrs. Joan said she hated shopping anyway. She referred a few other people to Momma and after awhile she was able to quit working at the hotel. That's not where the money came from though. Mrs. Joan waited until the last minute to ask

Momma to find a gown for a Mardi Gras ball. After two weeks of searching, Momma had to make her dress. Mrs. Joan couldn't believe it and had no idea that Momma could sew the way she did. About eight months after Momma had been working for Mrs. Joan, she came by our house with a business proposition. I was listening in from the other room.

"Sandra dawlin'," Mrs. Joan drawled. "I've talked with Lyle (that's her husband) and he wants to give me the money to open my own boutique showcasing your designs, but with my name on the label of course. I've wanted a boutique all my life," she went on, "and you're going to work for me. Isn't this great?"

I was smiling so happy, this was just the break we needed. Or so I thought until Momma started handling business.

"Really, tell me more," Momma said in that voice I knew meant she was about to say, "no".

"Well, we put up the front money. The building, materials and you design and make all the outfits and make ten percent off of each sale."

Momma stood up, found a sheet of paper and began scribbling some numbers down. After a minute she looked up and said, "No thank you."

Just like that, no sugar, no salt. Mrs. Joan was livid. "What? This is a great opportunity for someone like you Sandra. Okay, fifteen percent."

Momma laughed. "No."

I could tell Mrs. Joan wanted to call Momma a word we weren't supposed to use, but she was smart enough to know her territory was on the other side of town.

"Sandra, please, do you know how much money we can make?"

"Well, I know how much you could make."

Mrs. Joan smelled success with Momma so she was willing to work something out.

"Tell me what you want Sandra?"

"Well, at ten percent commission, working over sixty hours a week, which I figured that's how many hours I'll have to put in. And, I'm making less than what I did at the hotel.

Now if I'm going to steal time from my children's life it's going to be profitable for us, not you. So, I propose, seven designs a month, that's about thirty hours a week, a 50/50 partnership with the option to buy you out in a year."

Mrs. Joan tipped her chair backwards she stood up so fast. "You plum silly Sandra."

"I don't need you Mrs. Joan. But you came here thinking I did. Now, that's my offer, take it or leave it."

"You don't have to get an attitude Sandra."

Momma laughed for the first time.

"You standing in my kitchen with your nose raised up to your hairline and I have an attitude?"

Mrs. Joan didn't like Momma getting smart with her. She snatched up her purse and left and mumbled, "you're too smart for your own britches gal."

I was kind of mad at Momma that night. I knew that money could move us out of the projects and we could have a better life. But, she told me something that night I'll never forget.

"Momma, why didn't you do what Mrs. Joan told you to do?"

"First of all baby, you better not let me find out you ease dropping on my conversations again."

"Yes Ma'am."

"Second of all Princess," she said, that's what she calls me now, "no one is interested in what's best for you if they telling you what to do. Mrs. Joan didn't ask, she told me what I was going to do and you just don't turn over control of your life into nobody's hands but God."

That made sense, God has gotten us through this far.

"And third, A lady like Mrs. Joan scared of her own ideas, so she takes people's misfortune to elevate herself because she won't tap into her own dreams. And, I just wasn't willing to let her waltz in here and try to steal mine."

"Momma, does that mean we shouldn't let people help us?"

"Oh no baby, that's not what I'm saying. It's some good

people in this world. But everybody in this world ain't good for you. You let people help you sweetie, but just know their motives. Pay close attention to what their heart says, not their words. See, Mrs. Joan, she's still going to open a boutique with or without me. She'll find someone else, because she thinks she onto something."

"I think I understand."

"Baby, stay close to people who want to share in your dreams and visions, not those who want to steal it. I probably shouldn't tell you this but its time you know. Don't ever be a happy nigger for nobody, black or white, and you'll never forget the color skin you in or the gift you are."

That was the first and last time I ever heard Momma use that word. After that we prayed, especially for Mrs. Joan. That really didn't make sense to me, but Momma said, "God says to pray for those who use and abuse you-they need it most."

I'm still learning about God, so some things aren't clear to me yet. Momma explained it like this. If I do something good out of the kindness of my heart and that person takes advantage of me, don't worry about it. She say some folks will think they getting over on you, some will even secretly laugh and call you stupid, but that's okay, keep praying. Because while they trying to use you, the devil is really using them and they need the most prayer. Our prayer for Mrs. Joan ended up blessing us, because a few months later, Aunt Caroline married her high school sweetheart, sold her beauty shop and sent Momma enough money to open her own shop using her name on the designs.

Bible Boy

Grant Carpenter is a smelly boy. I mean stinky. He thinks he's a man too and he's just ten years old. Always has something smart to say and likes to debate with the Sunday school teacher. I thought we were poor, but Grant's parents are real bad off. But they don't seem to mind much, always smiling, always praising the Lord more than anybody. But I know they don't have much money, most Sundays they wear the same clothes over and over. And the church is always donating from the benevolent fund to help with their utilities. Momma made them some clothes and they told her the Lord would bless her for it. Now that I think about it, I don't know where Momma got extra money for material to make all those clothes she gave them, but she did. I understand now, God must provide for everybody, not just us. Anyway, I hate that Momma made me assist Mrs. Lyman, after her assistant left our church, but Momma says I should always be willing to do the Lord's work. I don't mind that so much, but I expect these kids to listen to me when I say things. I'm fourteen and still a child myself, but they are baby kids. Most of them listen though, except Grant.

His Momma, Mrs. Eileen told Mrs. Lyman, "I hope Grant doesn't give you too much trouble in class. He's, umm, well, different...special."

I know for a fact Mrs. Lyman lied in church because she told Mrs. Eileen that Grant didn't bother her. She lied because every time he corrects her on a scripture, which is often, she mumbles something under her breath that I know God wouldn't say and in the church at that. I told Momma about it, hoping she'd get mad at Mrs. Lyman and take me out of her class, but she didn't. Told me to respect my elders and just laughs when I tell her about Grant. Everybody in the church thinks he so cute and adorable. He bad, that's the only thing I know about him. I can't understand how he knows so much about scriptures though at ten, but he does. I wanted to tell Momma he must have an angel that comes too, but to keep peace, I didn't bring it up. But, that's the only way to explain it. Last Sunday, Mrs. Lyman was talking about marriage and the Lord must have caught my hand because I was ready to hurt Grant because his narrow tail told everyone he was going to marry me one day and all the kids laughed.

Anyway, Mrs. Lyman was saying, "God's word says that a husband is to respect his wife and a wife is to love her husband, because they are a team. And, that it's okay sometimes if a wife does whatever she wants without her husband's permission at times."

Grant stood up, that's how he does when he's about to correct her. He just stands up like a preacher man and I believe I saw a gray hair in that boy's head the other day. Maybe I didn't because Momma's old and she don't have gray hair yet. But Grant stood up with that look that belongs on an old man, (Momma calls its wisdom, I say it's foolishness) and said,"Do not be deceived. God is not mocked; for whatever a man sows..."

"Grant sit down," Mrs. Lyman stood up and yelled a little too loud in the church house. She kind of scared me. And even though Grant got on my nerves, he reminded me of the angel in my dreams when he spoke, soothing and calm.

"I apologize if I upset you Mrs. Lyman," he said, "but if you will go with me to Ephesians chapter five, I can assure you that your assessment is ..."

"Grant Carpenter, sit down, right now, do you hear me?" Mrs. Lyman said between her teeth.

He sat down and just looked at me, no smile, just that look. I rolled my eyes at him. Then he mouthed the word, "Pineapple," that's what he calls me, says I'm a hard shell with sweet meat on the inside. He just makes me want to scream. In fact I did and made Mrs. Lyman mad at both of us. But do you see what I'm talking about? He's too busy for a ten-year old if you ask me. I told Momma about it that night and she bent over laughing. Before I went to bed we read the chapter he mentioned and from what I can tell Grant knew what he was talking about...AGAIN!

Something You Don't Know

Excuse me. But I'd like to cut in here. I'm Grant. I hope you will indulge me for a minute. You should, I'm older than Malena when she started this story. I just want to set the record straight. I am ten years old, but not your typical ten year old child. Malena knows a lot but not everything about me and neither do you, yet. I'm young enough to know that my wisdom is not by accident, so let me explain. I have two fathers, one in Heaven and one here on earth. They both talk to me *all* the time. Yes, both of them. I am sure of two things; The Father, The Son and The Holy Ghost, and the fact that I love Malena Dawson. Now, where did this wisdom stem from? My mother told me that she read the entire Bible to me while I was in the womb and when she wasn't reading my Daddy was.

Initially, they read and prayed a lot because we are were poor. We still have very little money and I do mean very little. People feel sorry for us all the time and they shouldn't because my family's faith is being strengthened every day and our character is being molded. We will succeed, the Lord has already revealed it to me so I don't worry about that right now. As I was saying, my mother read me the Bible and as strange as it sounds I remembered it from early on. My parents said as a baby when I cried if they read the Word to me it would soothe me to silence. Around age four, I started hearing God speak to me and was reading and meditating on the word proficiently by seven. Right now, I can see light or dark around people and tell you if they're good or bad. Like Mrs. Lyman, her light is not that bright which is probably why she doesn't like me that much. Now, Malena, that girl is glowing and I'm attracted to it-even now.

Some of you will think I'm foolish and that may mean that your light is a little bit dim, but I don't worry about pleasing people, I already know my life is to please my Father in heaven. I have fun and play a lot with the rest of the kids in our neighborhood. I eat ice cream, candy, have to clean my room, wash dishes and everything else, but I'm happiest when I'm just in my room at night with God, just listening to what He's saying, thinking about it and talking to Him.

Being in His presence is something I can't put into words to you. The love is awesome. God is my best friend. Now, some kids make fun of me, others don't. I don't mind being called Bible boy except when people use it to put me down. I feel sad for them, because they're not hurting me but themselves and don't even realize it. So, instead of fighting about it-I pray for them. I like being happy and marvel in the fact that this is one house God will never have to knock to get into.

And what God doesn't reveal, my daddy teaches me. My Daddy and I are close and he too shares in my joy of the Lord. He's raising me as a boy, yet, preparing me to be a man. My daddy has a sixth grade education and yet he's the smartest man I know. My mother graduated from high school but didn't go any further. They married at eighteen and their love is like ointment in my life. I know I will share that kind of love-one day. Other than that, my life is similar to Malena's in terms of siblings. I have a sister, Faith, she's one. I love all the women in my life. And you can bet at ten, I know more about love than most. Mainly, that God is love and people need to stop taking that so lightly. I'm going to let her take back over now I'm headed to the natatorium to swim. I am still a kid, remember? But I know I'll see you again. Our story is not finished yet. Bye for now.

Sweet and Sour Sixteen

I went out on my first date this year, with Cedric Monroe. He plays football, basketball and runs track. All the girls like him, but he finally asked me out. We started out just talking, before we became an official couple. He walks me to all my classes, sits with me at lunch, and meets me after cheerleading practice, which is so superficial at times. It's certain people we can and can't talk too, can you believe that? I think that's kind of snooty and Momma told me, "don't be ignorant and let those girls change who you are." So, I talk to everybody doesn't matter to me.

Oh, back to the date. Cedric took me to dinner at a real restaurant, not McDonald's, and gave me my first kiss when he brought me home. I was so embarrassed when he put his tongue in my mouth. It felt weird and soggy and he kept wiggling his tongue like a guppy, in and out real fast. Not sure how much of that I'll be doing. I plan to remain pure until my wedding night. I made the mistake of telling him that when he revealed he wanted to really show me how much he loved me. Let's just say, he dropped me so fast-I didn't know what to do. He stopped talking to me and had another girlfriend before the week was out. So, that was my first entrance into the dating game.

To make matters worse Momma is seeing some man that she refers to as 'oh, that's just Mr. Sam baby', but I know he's more than that. He grins too much if you ask me, doesn't say much-just grins. I feel like I'm losing her because they spend a lot of time together now. Mitch and I are still close, but he has his own friends and can't think about anything but college. So, I sort of feel alone and rejected.

I remember Daddy saying, "When it seems no one else is around-God is always with you-just waiting for you to talk with Him-that's why He created you to fellowship with Him. So, I started sitting in my room talking with God and one day peace entered my heart and the situation and I noticed that Cedric wasn't that cute, just the star athlete at school. When he noticed I wasn't wet eyed over him anymore he wanted to talk. We did, I even had lunch with him a few times. When he needed help with his studies I assisted him, even bought a book of raffle tickets he was selling for his athletic club. One day during lunch, he asked me out again. I said no.

He said with a smirk, "Why? You know you're crazy about me."

"No, actually I'm not."

"Yeah right, then why you always doing things for me like you want me?"

I smiled. "That's the way I was raised Cedric. I don't have time to hold grudges. I never imagined you were asking for my help to get over on me."

"Well, that's...I just thought..." he said with space between his words.

"Yeah, I know what you thought."

It's amazing after Cedric realized that I didn't want him-his interest in me increased, but it was too late. He'd already shown his true nature and couldn't be trusted. I just remember both my parents saying, no matter how bad people hurt you, and some will, never let them change who you are in your heart. So, Cedric had no way of knowing whether I liked him or not, because I never allowed the situation to change regardless of his insensitive behavior. I finally managed to get past all that and felt good about myself until the day I came home from school and found Momma was sitting at the table crying.

"What's wrong, Momma?" I asked, rubbing her hair from the sticky tears on her face.

She looked up at me and told me to sit down. But, just that look on her face told me I wanted to stand in case I needed to run.

"That was Pastor Simms on the phone. Mrs. Mable died this morning."

Didn't I tell you I might need to run, because I sure did. I didn't have a destination in my head-I just ran. In all the years we never lost touch with Mrs. Mable. She came for a visit every Summer and Christmas and we spoke with her every Sunday after church. We were really the only family she had. Mrs. Mable and her pecan pies. Momma finally caught me and just held me in her arms while I cried until I couldn't cry anymore. I didn't want to go back to Ft. Knoxville, but Momma said we had to go say bye. We traveled that long highway back to the country. I was surprised to see Pastor Simms still preaching. He's about as old as the wood in the church now. It was a sad day though. I knew what that box was now and knew I wasn't going to see Mrs. Mable again anytime soon. I cried deeply as I stood over that box and called her grandma for the first time-she was gone to glory.

The Carpenters Jumping Ship

I started, "Momma, may I...never mind."
I didn't even bother to ask Momma if I could make a peanut butter and jelly sandwich because I knew she would say no. If it were up to me, I would eat them everyday, all day, but Momma says, "girl, you can't live off those sandwiches, you have to eat food," and, I knew we were waiting for the Carpenters.

The table was set with fresh cut flowers and hors d'oeuvrs scattered nicely on Momma's silver platter. The only thing missing were the guests of honor. A month after our return from Ft. Knoxville, Mrs. Eileen announced at church that she and her family were moving to California because her husband David had found a job out there doing construction work. I don't think I've seen Momma this sad in a long time. She and Mrs. Eileen have grown so close. Grant's still the same, he doesn't bother me as much, still stares, but I can deal with that. He hangs around Mitch a lot more when they come over. I normally sit and play with Faith and watch her blow spit bubbles through her bottom lip.

"Malena, hand me a napkin off that table please."

I was thinking, which I find I do a lot more lately. I didn't notice Momma crying. I didn't probe and ask what was wrong, I knew what it was. She's said some time ago about Mrs. Eileen, "friends like that are rare."

Mrs. Eileen felt the same, you could tell. I think Momma saw a lot of what she and daddy use to share in Mrs. Eileen and Mr. David. I never truly thought about it, but Momma didn't have a lot of friends. She was too busy taking care of us. And with the exception of Mr. Sam, Mrs. Eileen was it. She had a few acquaintances in church, but nothing major and Aunt Caroline was still living in Chicago with her family. I felt sad for Momma. But just as soon as she stepped into those tears, she came out. I wondered though.

"Momma, is Mrs. Eileen your best friend?"

"The best baby, the best."

"Are you hers, too?"

"No."

Wait a minute, I don't like the sound of this, sounds like Momma getting the short end of the stick.

"If she's your best friend, why aren't you hers?" I asked with somewhat of an attitude.

"Malena, her husband is her best friend, as well he should be."

I couldn't see being best friends with a boy and told Momma so.

"Princess, you better pray whoever you marry is your best friend, like your daddy was mine, after God of course."

"Like I said, I can't see being best friends with a boy."

Momma looked over her shoulder at me, wiped her hands off on the dishtowel by the sink and sat down at the table. I knew by the look on her face, she was about to give me yet another life lesson.

"Malena, let me tell something. I've had this talk with your brother because he's older and I know he's leaving soon."

"Oh no," I said in my head, "Momma, I'm not ready to talk about sex yet."

She laughed, giggled at me rather. "Baby, that talk is coming but just not today, we're talking about friends," she said still laughing at me, "but I told Mitch about sex too."

I didn't say a thing, wasn't surprised and I'm sure it didn't bother Mitch. He probably had a notebook out and a few questions already prepared. He and Momma had a different kind of closeness than she and I shared. I *was* a Daddy's girl and he's a Momma's boy, but she's made sure he knew to drop that apron string as soon as he gets married. Yes, I'm still eavesdropping occasionally, so I heard that conversation, but she doesn't know it.

"What I want to say Malena, the man you marry, make sure he's your friend, your best friend."

I just shook my head, still can't imagine talking to a boy about shopping, menstrual cycles...just can't see it.

"There will come a day when you look upside your husbands head and you'll know you love him, but when he makes you mad, and he will, you better hope you like him."

"Daddy never mad you mad?"

"Oh yes he did. But I couldn't stay mad at him for long because I would miss talking with my friend. I didn't just love him, I liked your Daddy-that's an important thing in a relationship-don't forget that."

I was a little shocked now because I didn't know my parents were ever mad at one another. I can remember a few times they were a little quiet, but never for long.

"I never knew Daddy made you mad," I finally said.

"And, you weren't supposed to. Grown folks arguments aren't meant for kids to hear, that's your responsibility as a parent to protect them."

Momma was about to say more when The Carpenters arrived. I got up to open the door and Mrs. Eileen welcomed me into her arms and hugged me like she always does-like she's known me forever. That moment I was sad because I was going to miss them too, even little Grant, who was there staring like he always does. He's calmed down, doesn't talk about the Bible as much unless you ask and he'll gladly discuss it. But his new Sunday school teacher lets him assist with her class. He knows that Bible that's all I can say. And before when I thought I saw a gray hair, it's visible now, more than one. At the rate he's going he'll have a white head before he's forty. It's strange how I miss this little boy already, I feel a sense of loss. He frustrates me, but he's like a brother—that must be what I'm feeling.

After dinner was over, we all sat around and laughed, played games and just tried to hold onto the moment for as long as we could. But the night came to an end and we began our goodbyes. I thought Momma and Mrs. Eileen were going to shake themselves into a seizure they were crying so hard. I couldn't help but feel their pain and I started to cry, too. It got to Mitch too, I know it did because he hugged Grant and Mr. David and went up to his room. I'm not going to let him know I saw the water in his eyes. The only person that wasn't crying was Grant. He was just standing back observing the entire scene. I walked over to him and asked for a hug. He gave me one, but I couldn't feel his little hands on me.

I told him, "I can barely feel your arms."

He smiled for the first time and said, "You never squeeze something as fragile as a heart too tight."

It was like he was hugging me but he wasn't. He pulled away from me and looked at me like he was troubled about something.

His little twelve-year old mind said, "Malena, whatever you do, don't ever lose your innocence. The light of love is upon you."

I couldn't say a thing and you know I like to talk. Grant is just a kid you know that, but he spoke like a man. I tell you that little boy is special in many ways.

A Wave of a Memory

The seasons changed and so did my memory. Funny how so much time has passed since we left Ft. Knoxville, ten years if you're still counting. Life has been so special in Biloxi. You know Mitch left for college last week, ended up going to Morehouse in Atlanta. I miss him so much, but I know life is about moving forward. I know Daddy would be proud of him because he sure took good care of us all these years.

The night before he left I gave him a present he says he'll cherish forever. You remember my Daddy's tote Bible, right? I decided Mitch should have it. I really think that's what Daddy would have wanted. I read it often, but Daddy had scriptures marked and notes that were meant for a man. Mitchell Darnell Dawson, Jr. had become just that—a man. My Momma has flourished into an elegant beauty and her boutique is thriving. I forgot to tell you before, but Mrs. Joan opened one too and it folded after the first year. Oh Mrs. Joan, funny ain't it? Momma called it right, didn't she? I'm old enough now to see what made my Momma so appealing to my Daddy all those years ago. It's more than her beauty. It's something deep inside of her. She's my Momma and my friend—though a mother first. It makes sense why Mrs. Mable was concerned about her spirit all those years ago. If you're fortunate enough to be around it for long, you know when it's no longer in your presence. You know something is missing. It's like a day with no sun and a night with no moon. Not right. That explains her pain behind Daddy's death. They were in love in the spirit, a place human emotions can't take you. Her spirit died with Daddy, but still had enough strength to bring her back to life. I understand that now that I'm older.

I wouldn't say I'm a woman yet because there's too much for me to learn about being a person first. I guess that's why I like to come to the beach that drew us here in the first place and try to catch a memory when I can, a memory of real people with pure hearts. I'm not sure why, but Ft. Knoxville doesn't seem so far away when I come here. I can see Daddy's smile in the sun, feel his embrace in the waves and smell Mrs. Mable's pecan pies in the breeze. I know, I have to move forward and walk towards my blessings now. That's what Momma worked so hard for. I guess its time to let Ft. Knoxville blow away in the wind-for good.

Just Me

I'm officially a woman now. Well, I'm eighteen. Age don't make me a woman just like good looks don't make you beautiful. I still look the same as I did yesterday. I'm not the same little girl you might remember, but I think I turned out okay. I grew some height...finally. I'm right at five foot eight, another inch over or under and I'd be awkard. I decided to cut my hair though, nice short crop. I love it. I had hoped I would have put some meat on my bones, but that didn't happen. Even with all Momma's fine cooking-my legs still look like a lead pencil. Yes, Momma can still throw down in the kitchen. She dropped that accent, but she sure didn't drop her culinary skills. Now, Mitch, the boy is huge, I mean huge. Not fat, just huge with shoulders made for a child to sit on.

Anyway, I'm procrastinating. I just wanted to let you know I'm leaving for college in a few days. I had several scholarships to choose from: Brown, Howard, Tulane, but for some reason I'm drawn back to the county, to Alcorn State University. I use to think it was because that's where Daddy wanted to go and by me going was like a gift to him. But it's something else; I guess I'll find out when I get there. So, I'm heading back to the woods to get an education. I've decided to major in Broadcast Journalism, so that should be interesting. You know I like to talk and tell stories so I have no doubt I'll fit right in. Anyway, I'll see you guys in a few years. Thank you so much for carrying me through my childhood.

PART II

Paper Dolls

The day is bright outside, but its dark in my heart. I came here to get an education and in two weeks I'm leaving with a degree, a best friend and shallow emotions. I've been too ashamed to tell you what's being going on with me the past four years. If I think too long about it, I'd say I've become someone I don't know anymore. I packed all that fine training Momma gave me in a suitcase about six months after I arrived here. First day here, I met Pamela Abrahms. I knew I had found a friend for life. Pam is a class A socialite from Georgia. Her parents fell into some money before she was born and kept falling until they started knocking on the door of rich. In so many ways, we're just alike, except her childhood wasn't interrupted by grief like mine.

She's beyond spoiled but I can't talk about her too much because Momma spoiled me too. I don't know if that's good or bad, but from where I'm sitting it's bad. It bothers me that my behavior is not *bothering* me enough to change it. And, believe me, it should. I guess I'm just too embarrassed to reveal some things to you. I'll put it like this: I ran across a few finish lines I had no plans to cross; sex, alcohol and outright siddity demeanor to name a few. And, the last time church saw me was when I went home for the holidays. And you'd think I never knew what a prayer was, because I haven't been doing that either. Unless I receive a letter from Grant…which is often. He's still a little boy in my eyes, but some of his letters read like prayers and they help, but not enough to make a difference. Mrs. Eileen calls to check on me, so I get a chance to talk with him occasionally. His voice has changed, sounds like a grown man with a deep timber to his tone. I have to remind myself, he's a kid. He still professes to love me, it's so cute, but again, he's still a kid. A kid with more sense than this man I'm dating. I was writing Grant back for awhile, but like a big sister to a little brother, but his affections continued to grow for me. I didn't think that was fair, so I just cut off all contact with him. I know that must have hurt, but what else could I do?

Amazing, before coming here my goal was to reach for the brass ring. Now I'm just reaching for rings with diamonds and rubies. Shameful, but it's the truth. I haven't had a serious boyfriend since I've been here because there are too many for me to date to be serious with one. For some reason I'm attracting older men, not sure why.

But just about every guy I've dated has been at least four or five years older. It bothered me at first, but I prefer an older man versus a younger one. Something foolish happens to a man when he's got an older woman. Anyway, I'm trying not to tell you too much. Because like I said earlier, I act like I don't remember a thing Momma taught me. And if sex makes you a woman, well, I'm a grown woman now that's for sure.

I haven't been too bad, but more than enough eyes have seen secrets only I should see in the bathroom and too many hands have dipped in places not meant to be displayed in public. I know I need to pray and ask God to forgive me, but I'm thinking, why, when I know I'm going to do it again. In fact, I'm waiting on Tony, a graduate student from Jackson, Mississippi right now. He's been my fix for the last six months. He's good too, sex feels good and I admit that. It hasn't felt right yet, just good. I don't know what right is supposed to feel like, but I know something is missing. But I tell you, Tony spends a lot of time and care trying to show me.

Shameful. And you can shake your head if you want, I'm just me being me and trying to be honest about it. I know now I want more from life than what I thought. Pam and I sit up some nights talking about it. The kind of men we're going to marry. No kids and no blue collar workers for us though. Our men have to be corporate or at least five rungs up on the ladder.

Pam wants her a dark chocolate man like herself, but I have a penchant for Café Au lait. Oh yeah, degrees, they have to have a degree to get our attention. And, he has to be an older man, at least by ten years and established because we can't waste our time with little boys anymore. We need someone who will compliment us.

So, see–that's why you haven't heard from me these past four years. I came here wide-eyed and innocent and leaving about as empty as those paper dolls I use to play with some years ago. Oh, I know this thinking is shallow. I just don't plan to spend my life struggling like Momma did those first few years. And I'm definitely not trying to wind up living back in the country either, so I'm just making sure it doesn't happen. Just another paper doll being handled and dressed by the hands of a stranger. Just another paper doll.

Troubled Waters

I hate to keep interrupting like this but once again I see Malena didn't bother to tell you a few things. Like the fact that my family and I came to her college graduation. She barely said two words to me when she saw me after *all* these years.

"Oh my goodness, look at you Grant," she said.

Okay, seven words. Can you believe that mess? She didn't hug me or anything. That man she was with had her in a vice grip, like she was going to float away if he took his hand off her. That bothered me so bad you just don't know. But, that's okay because I know she's caught up already in the things of this world. I felt it happening. I'm still a little kid in her eyes, but she's going to see one day--the truth. It's only so long you can toss around nonsense before it hits a wall. Right now, she's straddling the fence between good and evil and if she doesn't slow down...well, I don't want to think about it, so I just pray for her.

How do I know this? I may work her nerves, but Malena was never rude or selfish. If nothing else, she at least thought of me as a little brother. The fact that she doesn't write or return a call tells me she's someone else. Because she used to have a heart that I see college life has stolen from her. I know you still think I'm a little boy too. But remember what I told you before, my parents raised me a boy while preparing me to be a man. And, I'll tell you this much. I'm man enough to know I would not have touched her the way she's been touched and you know what I mean. She's lost her innocence. She's a grown woman and I know that. But, a man would wait if he loved her. HE WOULD WAIT! But like I said, she's caught up and can't see. It seems she did two things on her twenty-first birthday, turned a year older and lost her natural born mind. But I still love her and that will never change.

Let me set the record straight. I don't expect her to be with me now by any means. I don't have a job and I'm still in high school. Our time is not yet. But I don't like watching her step out of order either and that's what she's doing. She's running, from what I don't know? If I had to guess, she's not running from me, but the God in me. I talk with my Father about it often—both of them.

One thing I'm sure of is that God is faithful. He's shined his light bright on this family since we left Biloxi. That's another reason I know Malena doesn't read my letters because she hasn't said a thing to you about how well my family is doing. The job my Daddy was offered in California fell through when we moved here. We were back to square one, worse actually. But we kept praying. About a month later Daddy found a job at a radio station as a janitor. By accident, or should I say a miracle ,the owner of the station, Ralph Bailey approached him. It seemed he'd watched my Daddy for over six months. So often he ignored my Daddy when he spoke to him in the morning and as often as he was rude to not only him, but others. Daddy always had a kind word or a smile for him. Mr. Bailey was curious and interested in finding out the secret to my Daddy's happiness. There he was a man of wealth and fortune for all intents and purposes, still not happy. Daddy was sweeping and mopping floors and was singing joyful praise when he didn't think anyone was listening. So, one day Mr. Bailey asked him,

"What on earth do you have to be so happy about all the time?" Daddy told him right there on the spot about Jesus and from that moment on they became fast friends.

Mr. Bailey later said he always felt something in Daddy that he knew was missing from his life but never thought it was the Lord. He knew he had everything money could afford him but no peace. Yet, he knew we had very little and Daddy radiated. Daddy, being Daddy, invited Mr. Bailey to church where he was eventually saved and gave his life to Christ. One night he was over for dinner when this thought came to him. He had this look on his face like he didn't know why he hadn't thought about it before. But he offered Daddy a job that changed our lives. He gave Daddy a chance to host his own thirty minute call-in gospel show on Sunday mornings. Now remember my Daddy didn't have an education, but he knew the Word of God. He agreed to do it on a trial basis and it was so well received it eventually expanded into an hour five days a week.

The money didn't just roll in—it floated in, making up for all the years we didn't have. And, on top of that, Daddy decided to go back to school and get his high school diploma. So we are doing very well. We have a nice house, cars and brand new clothes, but we're still grounded and thankful for everything, good and bad. Funny thing is, the more money we made the harder we prayed as a family—not to be fooled by the riches or forget where they came from. Now, I'm sure Malena's Momma or Mitch has mentioned it to her too. But, like I said, the girl is CAUGHT UP! So, I have to wait until our time comes because she's been touched, but she hasn't been loved and she won't be until she's touched by me. For now, I have to continue to yield to what God is telling me to do in order to be where I should be when destiny prevails.

Off Key-letter

My life has become like an out of tune piano. The keys are still making a lot of noise, but not producing any beautiful music. I turned twenty-four yesterday in case you're wondering. After graduation Pam and I moved to Atlanta and we share a condo in Buckhead. I hadn't planned to move here, but it just sort of happened that way. Plus, Mitch is living here now. He never left after graduating from Morehouse. He's still Mitch and has become our Daddy all over again with his new wife, Stacey and son, Mitchell III. It's sweet to see him keeping Daddy's name alive. I'm happy for him because he seems so happy. I have a wonderful job at a news station, WBNT, as the weekend anchor and reporting the news three days a week. My ratings are great and if I have my way I'm going to have the weekday evening broadcast in another year. The viewers love me and I've made several friends here. I'm content with life. At least that's what I tell myself. I've done really well for myself. I know, I said that already. I ramble when I can't make sense out of things. I guess what I'm trying to say none of this is what I thought I wanted. I'm living a life I'm not even sure is mine, but I won't do anything to change it. For instance, tonight I had planned to go to church for the first time in five months. But instead, I'm going to a party with Pam. And the sad thing is I know I *need* to be in church. I'm trying to pray again though, but it doesn't seem real. Flat to be honest. Momma thinks I go every Sunday, but I just can't seem to make it anymore. It's hard getting up for eleven o'clock service when I don't get in from the club until five in the morning and you may as well know I have a man--so you know I'm not going straight to bed when we get here. I'm not out there like you think. I've dated several men since I've been here, but he's the first one that I slept with, so close your mouth.

I've been with him two years now. How can I describe Mark? Well you already know my requirements and he met them all; established chemical engineer who's twenty years my senior. He makes me laugh, takes good care of me and he looks and smells good. I don't know how much longer I can stay with him though. It's still not right and lately it's been *very* different. Different in the sense that I find myself sick afterwards and I mean literally. To the point of throwing up and dry heaving. I try to hide it from him but he's not crazy so he finally asked me what was wrong after about the fifth time it happened. When I came out of the bathroom he was sitting there with this look of concern on his face.

He gave me sort of a lazy grin and said. "Malena, is there something I should know?"

My head was heavy, heavy and my stomach felt hot, like fire.

"Like what?"

"Like, are you pregnant?"

If I wasn't sick before, I was about to be, because that idea repulsed me. I've made up my mind, no kids—ever. But I didn't tell him that because the idea of a pregnancy seemed pleasing to him.

"Mark, no, I'm not pregnant. Think about it, a condom and birth control pills?"

He looked sad for a minute. "I forgot about that."

I don't know how he did, because the only major fight we

had was over me not having sex with him when we were both out of condoms. He tried to reason with me by saying, "Malena, you on the pill and you know I've been tested, this is ridiculous."

"Mark, you can walk in here with the surgeon general, whatever you want. No condom, no nothing else."

He stormed out after that, I thought he was going home, but he came back an hour later with condoms, temper cooled off and loins on fire.

"So, if you're not pregnant, what is it, because you're starting to give a brother a complex."

I kissed his cheek, his face and wrapped myself up in his arms and just told him, "I'm probably stressed Mark. I wouldn't worry about it."

He didn't because that gave him the go ahead to touch me in my secret places.

You'd think I would stop sleeping with him, but I haven't. I'm almost positive I know what it is, which is why I know I need to go to church as I said before. I'll just give it to you like Momma gave it to me in Cancun last year for my birthday.

"Malena, you're grown, taking care of yourself and I'm proud of you."

I knew by her tone she wasn't exactly about to praise me for my achievements when she chose to look out over the water instead of at me.

"I get the feeling you're trying to move too fast," she said.

"I'm fine Momma, just working hard trying to make a name for myself."

She took a sip of her virgin strawberry daiquiri she was holding in her hand and said, "Yeah, I know. I just hope you're making the right kind of name."

I raised up out my seat. I was mad because I didn't like the implication of her tone.

"What's that supposed to mean Momma?"

"You know exactly what it means. Don't be down there opening your legs up to any and everybody."

She said it just like that with an attitude, but when have

you ever known Momma to hold her tongue? I stood up so fast I knocked my chair backwards. I was really hurt that she would think that. She just looked at me with this smirk on her face and said.

"What you think you bout to do?"

"Momma, I don't appreciate you calling me a slut."

She smiled. "That's not what I said Malena."

"Don't spread my legs open for everybody. How am I supposed to take that?"

"You can take it sitting your butt down and bring that tone with you."

Now, I'm a grown woman, but I can tell you right now, the lovely Sandra Wilkes Dawson was about to take me out. So I decided to sit down like she suggested.

"Listen Malena. Now you know I'm not one of those Momma's that want to control my kids life."

"I know that Momma. I know that. But…"

"Let me finish," she said cutting me off, "you can do what you want, but whatever you do you should have fun doing it."

"I am having fun, I love my job, I love Georgia and I like my man."

"Oh, I don't doubt that, but you just don't look happy baby. And after two years you just *like* this man, you don't love him?"

"As a friend yes, but that's it and we're both okay with it."

"If he's just a friend you shouldn't be sleeping with him."

See, she did it again, still no sugar, still no salt after all these years.

"Momma."

"Malena, do you want a husband some day?"

"No, not really, not anymore. I just want a successful career, make a name for myself like I said earlier."

"You ever want any kids?"

"No! Defintely no."

She laughed. "Do you want love in your life Malena?"

"Of course I do."

"Then don't block yourself from receiving it baby."

"I'm not. I just haven't found that 'one' yet. Love is not as easy as it was when you and Daddy met."

"Yes it is sweetie, your spirit just has to be open to receive it. And I know how I raised you with the Word. The Word is in your spirit even when you fight against it, it's fighting for you. It will convict you if you doing something you don't have any business doing."

"And that means?"

Momma took my hands in hers and just looked at me for a second.

"It means that your spirit will reject what's not supposed to be in you, Malena. You follow me? It will not accept it, I'm telling you what I know and had to find out myself the hard way. Now, you can fight against it and drive yourself crazy, sick or whatever. but, it's going to come up and out somehow."

"Well, I don't know about all that Momma."

"You're not going to church anymore are you?"

"Yes." That lie slipped out before I could catch it.

"You reading your Bible?"

"Yes." Lie number two, shall I go for three?

"Mitch says you haven't been to church in months."

"I don't go to his church anymore."

She just looked at me like she was disappointed. I wasn't good at lying and she wasn't good at accepting one or should I say three of them.

"I'm going to take a nap," she said. "But remember what your Daddy and I taught you and your brother about stealing."

I stayed up all night trying not to remember anything Daddy taught me, the way he looked or talked. Because see I can pretend I don't know right from wrong, but his words came back so powerful that night as if he were sitting next to me. "Never steal anything that doesn't belong to you. That includes someone's time, their emotions, their trust and lastly, don't steal God's time because that truly doesn't belong to you."

So you can see why I've started praying again because Lord knows I need God to save me, because I definitely can't save myself, not at the rate I'm going. And I'm terrified because I know I am on a path of self-destruction.

Maybe it's Time

Those eyes I saw on my graduation and denied myself the pleasure to admire turned twenty-one today. I couldn't accept them then because I calculated in my head fast that Grant was considered a felony in most states. Mrs. Eileen always said he was special and he is. I'm so proud of him. He accelerated in high school graduating with honors at sixteen and received his bachelor's degree in Economics from Stanford in three years. He's working at the radio station alongside his father since Mr. Bailey has retired and left everything in their hands. The man is special I keep telling you. If you're wondering if I went to his graduation, I didn't. I couldn't get off from work. Well, I could have but Grant doesn't know that. He said he understood when we spoke. I'm glad he did because there was no legitimate reason for me not to attend. But that's the way he is-understanding. I can't buy that from anyone I know.

Pam said, "he's just a punk kid girl, don't lose your focus, that boy can't offer you nothing but a piece of candy and a two second roll in the sack. He's toooo young for you." That comment from her created silence between the two of us for over a week.

I didn't appreciate her or anyone for that matter saying

negative things about him. Any woman in her right mind would be honored to have a man like Grant in her life. I guess I haven't been in my right mind because I haven't spoken with him since I broke up with Mark, and that was six months ago. I didn't think Grant would be home but I decided to try anyway. I was about to hang up after the third ring when I heard him.

"Hello," he answered in a husky, somewhat rushed tone.

"Happy Birthday," I said in the most cheerful voice I could muster.

But for some reason I was nervous. Okay shaking, whatever.

"It is now," he said.

It sounded like he was resting and raised up when he heard my voice.

"So, how's it feel to be a year older?"

Even I know that's the most lame question of the decade but I couldn't think of anything else to say.

"I feel good. Blessed."

Silence.

"So, what's on your mind Malena?" he asked breaking the stillness of the air. "I get the feeling you're not just calling to wish me a Happy Birthday."

"Listen at you. Turned a year older and bolder."

"I guess the question is, am I old enough for you yet?" he said in a challenging sort of tone.

"Actually, your birthday is not the only reason I called. I've been thinking."

"About?"

I closed my eyes and went for it. "About why I haven't been able to get you off of my mind this past year."

"You figured it out yet?" he asked.

It was clear he wasn't going to make this easy at all.

"Not really, I'm hoping you can help with that."

I think I heard him laugh before he said, "Bottom line baby, we are connected."

"You're so sure about that."

"Malena, even when I'm not with you, I'm with you. It's

always been that way. You feel it too you just haven't accepted it."

"I don't know if its that cut and dry Grant."

"Then why did you call here?"

"To wish you a Happy Birthday."

"And?"

"To find out what you wanted…"

"For myself or my birthday?"

"Both."

"YOU!"

"You don't mince words do you?"

"I don't have the time. It's always been you. Even when you were rolling your eyes in Mrs. Lyman's Sunday school class, it was you."

"Grant…"

"My question to you, are you ready to take this to the next level?"

"Yes, but…"

"But what, Malena?"

"I'm ready Grant, honestly I am. But, I do have a few concerns."

"Like?"

"Well, you're an adult now, but you are younger than I am. I just wonder how my colleagues will look at me, people will talk."

"Malena, you think I'm worried about what people have to say. I don't live my life for that and neither should you."

"Grant, that's easy for you to say, you're not the one that has to deal with it."

"So, you're not ready after all?"

"I am."

"You can't be, not for me. Not with that kind of thinking. Don't open a door you're not prepared to walk through yet Pineapple."

"I wish you'd be a little more understanding about this, Grant."

"I understand that you'd rather live your life for this

world than for yourself. That kind of thinking is shallow Malena and you know it."

"Grant, I have people who look up to me and I just don't want them talking. That's all I'm saying."

"Let them talk. They're going to do it anyway, whether you're with me or somebody else, you know that."

Grant had a point, because folks had things to say about Mark being older than I was. They called him a cradlerobber.

"I wish I had your beliefs."

"Malena, since you've known me, my steps have being ordered by the Lord and always will be. Because come judgement day, and it will come, I don't want to be held accountable for missing out on any gifts God has for me because I was worried about people who can't save me at the last hour."

"I guess I can't argue with you."

"You have a choice. We both do. So I ask again, are you ready to see where this is going?"

"Yes. I'm ready."

"Good, I've been waiting a long time for you, woman."

The Next Two Weeks

For the first time in forever, I felt like my old self again pre-college, pre-corporate world. I forgot that I had forgotten how to laugh, to relax and just embrace life. Grant and I stayed up every night talking into the wee hours of the morning. Some nights I was lucky if I got three hours of sleep, but my body was operating on a different kind of energy. We talked about everything and sometimes nothing at all. Even in silence across the miles our words were heard in the deepest part of our hearts. But one of the most romantic things he did was prayed with me every night before we ended our conversation. My spirit just started coming to life again. I began to realize that I was walking in the ways of this world and not in the spirit as I had been raised to do. It was refreshing to find someone to share that old part of myself with. I remember a few times I asked Pam if she wanted to go to church, her response was. "For what?"

"I just think we should occasionally give thanks, don't you?"

"Girl, I'm doing fine. God must be looking out for me, so why bother. I can have church right here sitting at my kitchen table."

"That's true, Pam. But, I just think we should be fellowshipping, you know. I mean does it ever bother you?"

"Nope," she said, "Look around, like I said, we must be pleasing God, He's been too good."

I didn't answer her, even though I knew in my heart that kind of thinking was wrong. But what did I do? Didn't go either and convinced myself that God understood and used that as my excuse not to go. I wasn't even sure God could still see my face like before with my behavior. But, Grant gave me hope that God is faithful and not just sometimes, but all the time. I was ashamed that I had allowed my life to go so long without acknowledging God as I should, but I was afraid and didn't know why. And I found myself sharing those things with Grant, things I hadn't told anyone else, including Pam.

After two weeks of connecting on a different level, Grant and I decided to make arrangements to see one another. He wanted to fly to Atlanta, but I chose to fly there because I wanted to see his parents and Faith. No one could have told me that I wasn't about to engage in the sweetest relationship with Grant. Well, no one except Valerie. I don't know her last name or how long she's been a part of Grant's life, but she made it clear he wanted nothing else to do with me when I called to give him my flight arrangements. I thought I had dialed the wrong number when I called his home one morning from the station.

On the second ring, a lady answered. "Hello."

I hesitated and finally said, "Hi, this is Malena Dawson calling for Grant Carpenter, is he available?"

"Oh, you, hold on a minute," she said nastily and slammed the phone down.

I'm thinking by this time, not only who is this woman, but I know she didn't just get an attitude with me. I could hear her whispering in the background with a man, a man that sounded like Grant and my heart dropped.

After about a minute she came back and said, "he's not here."

"Not there? Okay. May I leave a message please?"

"You can leave whatever you want, but I can't *make* him

call you back."

I had to take a deep breath before saying. "I didn't ask you to make him do anything, just asked that you take a message. And may I ask who I'm speaking to."

"Valerie," she said like I was supposed to know who she was. "Do or don't you have a message for Grant."

Okay, sistergirl is going just a bit too far for me this morning. "Who are you?"

"Since he won't tell you, I will. I'm his girlfriend and I don't appreciate you..."

I had to cut her off.

"What? You just ask Grant to return my call."

I heard someone whisper in the background then and she laughed and finally said, "Look, Grant doesn't want to see you and said don't call him again," and she hung up the phone in my ear.

I don't know how I managed to make it through the rest of my day, but I did. I've grown accustomed to faking a smile in front of a camera, but I was garnering Oscar status today. I made it home and every tear I had been holding back exploded. To make matters worse, Pam was home from work early and I had to contend with her. I gave her the short version of what happened. Since she wasn't one of Grant's biggest fans to begin with she had plenty to say.

"Girl, I told you to leave that little boy alone. He's playing games."

"Pam, I'm not up for the 'I told you so's if you don't mind."

"What are you're going to do?"

"I don't know Pam. I need to talk to him and find out what's going on?"

"Talk with him, after what he did?"

"Pam, this is not like Grant. You don't know him."

"I know another woman answered his phone claiming to be his girlfriend, so one of you getting played or both."

I was too tired to argue. I went into my room and crawled into bed. I felt...I don't know how to tell you. I felt like more than an idiot and not quite a fool. I couldn't help think Grant was paying me back for all those years I pushed him away, but even that didn't sound right to my mind. But I had to look at the facts, another woman answered his phone and it sounded like she belonged there. I turned the ringer off on my phone, said a prayer and cried myself to sleep. A voice I had not heard in over fourteen years, but remembered like it was yesterday woke me from my sleep saying, "Daughter of mine, go forth."

Pushed

I finally stopped trying to reach Malena after a month of her not accepting my calls. It's a lonely feeling to come home every night checking my caller ID to see if she had called. My patience is being put to the test, because it's taking everything in my power not to be angry with her. If she wasn't ready, that's fine, but to just drop the ball like she did was downright cruel. I talked with Mitch to see if he knew what was going on and he didn't know anymore than I did. He said,Malena just told him that she'd made a mistake and we both needed to move on with our lives.

Now she's pulled some stuff, but to call us a mistake cut hard. It made me wonder who I'd been talking with the past few weeks. I decided the best thing for me to do was to leave her alone. I prayed about it and now I'm just waiting on God to remove these feelings from my heart. I don't need this from her, or any woman. But I'd sure feel better if I knew what was going on. The only thing I can think of is she got scared. One minute she was supposed to call with flight arrangements and then nothing. I tried calling her and she never answered the phone that night and wouldn't take my calls at the station.

It was insane. I talked about it with Kendrick, one of the

brothers from church who was staying with me at the time. He moved in for about a month to keep from signing another lease on his apartment for a year because he's getting married. He and his fiancée, Valerie, had plans to buy a home, but until then he was moving into her place after the wedding. But he didn't have any advice when we talked about it a week after the incident.

"What do you think happened, Carpenter? I mean you two were onto something."

"Brother, I think Malena needs a challenge and I don't have time to give her one. Not when ultimately she's going to get the man I am now."

Kendrick just shook his head, he had his own problems and I knew that. I guess I should count myself fortunate.

"If she needs a challenge man, I can't help her. Life is too short for games. I can't offer her that."

I meant that and Kendrick knew it because that's why he was in the situation he was in at age twenty-nine. He started chasing behind Valerie a year ago. That sister took him through a loop and a hoop. Personally, I don't see what he sees in her in the first place (but I'm not the one marrying the girl), because she has the nastiest, and I do mean nastiest, disposition I've ever seen on anyone. But, he told me he had to have her at the time. Kendrick finally admitted he was playing that spirit/flesh game and his flesh won. Well, it turns out she just liked being chased and he liked chasing and that little game landed them engaged. Happy story, right? Wrong. He told me the week before the wedding, "Grant, I'm engaged to marry a woman I can't stand and don't know how to get out of this mess."

"What you mean you don't know how to get out? Tell her."

"It's not that easy."

"Man, this is the rest of your life you talking about."

"Well, we can get a divorce if it doesn't work out."

"Now you know that's not an attitude to take going into a marriage. It sounds doomed from the offset."

"I know, but, we've got all this stuff planned, spent all this money, folks coming into town."

"Man, you said you can't stand this woman, not she has some problems you need to get past. Or, is it cold feet?"

He looked up at me like he was being sentenced to prison or something.

"I'm not scared. I'm ready to get married and she does have some good qualities, but, she's not the one and I know this."

"Look, I don't know what to tell you other than marriage is not something to take lightly."

"I know, I don't know what I'm going to do man."

He married the girl. That's how he decided to handle the situation. And I'm here to tell you it was the saddest wedding I have ever attended.

Like I said earlier, I don't have time to do anything other than be myself. I know in my heart I was prepared to go all the way with Malena, but she'll never know, because she pushed too far this time, too far.

Justified

Patrice was waiting at the radio station when I arrived at work. Patrice Cumming I've been seeing her about three months now. I kid you not, that's the lady's last name. And she makes it painfully obvious that she would like to hear it roll off my tongue in the heat of passion.

"Granttttt," she says running into my arms and planting a moist kiss on my mouth.

"Hi Patrice," I said a bit uncomfortable by her public display of affection. "What you doing here?"

"Well, I was thinking you should come over for dinner tonight and you know."

I know, what her, 'you know' meant and I wasn't down with it. Don't get me wrong, I like the girl. I can't help it. She's smart, beautiful to look at and a body built to destroy if you let her. I just can't afford to let anything happen, because I know where my heart belongs still. I never told you I didn't get tempted, because I am a man you know. But, it has never bothered me that I haven't been intimate sexually with a woman yet. I pride myself on the fact that I'm waiting to be with that one woman.

Some of my boys give me a hard time about it, the ones

that know. The rest of them think I'm out there or assume I'm wearing myself down in sex. But I say again, it has not been easy. I find myself praying often to release this sexual desire off of me. Some days I'm fine; others I'm not. And, it doesn't help that sex is everywhere nowadays. In fact it's standing here in front of my face, so to Patrice's invite, I say, "What time?"

"Seven."

"I'll be there."

And that's where I am, standing inside her home smelling the aroma of salmon, perfume and sex with a bit of soft jazz stirring it deeper into the air. I can see it in her eyes…she wants me. And, tonight, I'm ready to let her have it. I can't help wanting her and I whisper that in her ear when she delicately rubs her body against mine. Malena is in my heart, but she's nowhere near my mind at the moment. She almost seems like a lost memory that's been sucked out by time, and the more Patrice touches me, the more she's lost.

"Follow me," Patrice says leading me over to the couch.

And I do just that, lowering myself down on top of her. I forgot why I came over here in the first place, then she pulled my sweater over my head and sucked the tip of my nipple into her mouth. The warmth of her mouth drove me insane and I let her know it by caressing every inch of clothing off of her until she was naked in my presence. She touched me bad, hard, and I was ready to slip and plant myself into her. I probably would have if she hadn't raised up and grabbed my face to look at me.

"Grant, I have wanted you so bad, for so long," she said looking in my eyes.

My eyes, her eyes, I did not know. There was no mirror of myself looking back, no recognition. My body went ice cold. I raised up off of her and she must have sensed something because she didn't try to stop me. I began putting my clothes on and I looked back at her and said, "I'm sorry Patrice. I can't do this."

She just stared at me like she understood, then started calling me some words that should never come out of woman's mouth. Those words hit me in the back like knives as I left her house. But there was no way I could go through with it. Like I said if I hadn't looked in her eyes I'd probably be repenting for this tomorrow morning. The weird thing, all my life it's been about Malena, waiting for Malena. Tonight it had little to do with her. Like I told you she was lost somewhere around the time Patrice's tongue was traveling down my chest towards my, well, I won't go into detail. But looking in her eyes I know in my heart there's got to be something empty about being inside a woman you don't love. And I wasn't willing to risk finding out what it was. So, I did the only thing I know how to do and that's pray. I must have thought my life was on the line because whatever desires were in me I placed on the mercy seat in desperation. What Patrice was offering, any woman for that matter, wasn't worth it. I'd come too far by grace to risk losing the anointing I know God has placed on my life.

Another Year

Mitch meant well, I know he did, but I'm not up for this birthday celebration tonight. I just want to go crawl back in my bed and stay there. I was about to pull off when he opened his front door and walked towards my car. Lately, between him and Momma they are starting to work my nerves. Oh yeah, I didn't get that job doing the weekday news. But I am hosting the a morning talk show. I hate the hours, but I love the job, minus the politics involved. I'm wearing myself out though with all these folks constantly snatching at me, wanting this, wanting that and I don't have a damn thing left to give sometimes. I'm sorry, I didn't mean to curse. As you can see, I'm just all over the place right now. I have everything, everything I said I wanted out of life. The perfect job, money, status and last year Pam and I each bought homes and I'm not in a Toyota, this is a Mercedes XL convertible I'm sitting in. That's why I dodge Momma now, she says, "Get back in church. You need Jesus,. That's what's wrong with you."

I was polite, never going to be rude to that woman, she's my Momma, and I know Jesus can get me out of this mess. I just feel like I've let God down. He lifted me up before and here

I am sinning again. It's hard to believe that God can still love me because I don't have much love for myself anymore. All these folks preaching to me--Momma, Mitch and Stacey. Well, they're not preaching, just worried and they probably should be. I'm just having a hard time believing these days. And every time I start to believe, I'm knocked back down again. I know my faith needs to be restored.

"You going to sit out here all night?" Mitch asked opening my car door.

I got out and he hugged me, like he was trying to erase some of the pain that went unsaid. I walked into his home and D3, that's what we call Mitch's son, stumbled towards me like a drunk man and raised his arms for me to pick him up.

Can someone tell me how it is a child can make you forget every stress and worry on your mind? Life made sense to me with him in my arms.

"Tee Tee," D3 said, just grinning a toothless smile that melted my heart. As fast as he jumped in my arms, he jumped out and took off running to destroy something in the house I'm sure. I followed Mitch into the den and my mouth opened. Stacey outdid herself; balloons, flowers and a big yellow cake with buttercream frosting. My favorite.

"I can't believe you did all this," I said, hugging her,.my spirits were lifting. There's nothing like family, and especially a family that loves you. And Mitch was right I needed this.

"We have a surprise for you," he said, handing me a Cosmopolitan, "sit down and relax."

He walked behind the bar and whispered something in Stacey's ear, she giggled and they disappeared into the kitchen. Like I told you awhile back, he's Daddy all over again. That made me smile seeing the two of them so happy. I have no doubt Daddy would be proud of him, now me, let's just say I doubt he'd still be calling me a Princess. I went back to Mark after the incident with Grant. It lasted about a month before I ended it for good. It felt too forced; like I was with him just to keep from being alone. And the memory of Grant didn't help the situation at all. So I've been good the past year, hurting, but good. I took the time to start going back to church more (not every Sunday) and praying, so that has kept me busy, but something is still missing.

Sometimes it sounds like a voice whispers to me, "pray, pray, pray."

Then I start feeling ashamed of myself and start thinking I've committed too many sins for God to hear me, so I just stopped. Other times, I feel a strong sense of peace around me. I was about to go looking for Mitch and Stacy when I felt a presence in the room, a calm that just lit up the area. I jerked around and there he was.

"It's been a long time," Grant Carpenter said in a voice that sounded like it bounced off the walls.

I knew who he was. Years had pulled him up to about six feet and stretched him to 200 pounds, but his eyes had not changed. Those eyes that have been in my heart the past year are looking at me now and won't loose me. And I don't want them to. How can I describe his eyes to you, not intense...disarming maybe? Yes, that's it, disarming.

I could feel my head shaking slowly from side to side and for a minute that's all I could do. I finally let something that was barely audible slip through my lips.

"You're really not a little boy anymore," I said more to myself, totally forgetting that I'm supposed to be mad at him for what he did to me, but I'm not.

He walked up on me and let the back of his forefinger trail the side of my face. I just closed my eyes and felt this warmth go through my body. His finger stopped at my chin and lifted it up to meet his eyes. Eyes that looked like they were scanning my face into memory.

"I was never a little boy, Malena Dawson," he said, as he took his other arm and lifted my entire body into his.

I don't know how long I stayed in his arms like that. I wasn't counting the time. I just know that night for the first time in forever, I felt safe again.

"You look great," I finally said.

"Thank you. So do you?" he said, looking down at me.

His arms were still around my body and I was in no hurry to walk out of them.

Looking at his face and into his eyes, I forgot why I hadn't spoken with him in over a year. He truly had grown from a little boy into a man. And as strange as it sounds, it didn't feel awkward to be in his arms. I had often wondered what it would feel like because it'd been years since I'd seen him last. But it hit me right then, this man was not a stranger. He was someone who'd known me over half my life.

Grant just looked at me and said, "Happy birthday Malena."

I blushed under his gaze, pulled him closer and said, "It is now."

Worth the Wait

I asked Mitch not to tell her I was coming to town. My thinking was she wouldn't respond to letters or phone calls, she wouldn't be in a big hurry to see me. I hadn't planned to come here, not yet anyway. I didn't realize how much I still hurt by her behavior, but after the incident with Patrice, I knew I still cared about her and I could never move on without confronting these feelings. All the worries left me when I saw her sitting there and I thanked God for her that moment. He had answered my prayers once again.

I hope you don't still doubt me. Did you not just read how that woman responded to me? I could have stepped out of order last year and come here, but everything is timing–God's timing. And this is just the beginning.

Just like Old Times

Well, not exactly like old times, because you all know I stopped giving Grant the time of day after the Valerie incident. No, I haven't brought it up yet, I was too happy to see him last night, but I will at some point. I'm waiting for him to pick me up from the station right now for lunch so we can pick up where we left off last night. His flight leaves tomorrow and I miss him already. I was missing him before he got here if that makes sense. I was still sitting on the set with my co-anchor, Walter Stiles, waiting to do a promo when one of the production assistance walked Grant in the studio. I'm here to tell you, my smile was brighter than the light shining on me. So much so, the cameraman had to get my attention and tell me to sit back, because I was about ready to jump out my seat.

"You like them young Malena," Walter said sarcastically.

Walter is twenty years my senior and has tried to get his size twelve in my front door since I've been here. I don't have a problem with Walter's age, just the wedding band on his left hand.

"Walter, it really doesn't matter how old they are if they're a man," I said, indicating he was anything but.

It hit me that moment my attraction to older men went back to Mrs. Lyman's Sunday School class, with the little boy who was younger than us all and had more wisdom than some of the grown men in church. I was looking for *older* Grants all over again and didn't know it. Even now sitting here looking at him, he doesn't look like a boy. He never did really. He's got this look. I still can't describe it to you. He just looks so intense and serious. But his smile is warming like it's meant just for you. And at twenty-two, the gray in his hair is evident. It's also his confidence, not cockiness, but that of a warrior, a protector. I'm almost in awe of him and the man that he's become. Grant truly lives his life to please God, without regard to what others think and that exudes from his inner being. I don't know that I ever want to find myself without him in my life.

I thought we were going to some fancy restaurant but Grant pulled into the park.

"May I hold your hand?" he asked when we got out the car.

I shook my head up and down, surprised that he asked, most men don't ask they just grab your hand assuming its available. After Grant spread out the blanket, I took a seat and kicked off my heels. I was trying to be cute, but I was hungry, too. And Grant was taking his sweet time taking the foiled sandwiches out of the picnic basket he had. He handed me what I thought to be a deli sandwich and to my surprise was a peanut butter and jelly, sandwich with the ends trimmed off.

"What's this?" I asked, smiling, "I haven't eaten one of these things since college."

Grant laughed at my amazement. Well, if you call it a laugh. It's more like the sound of a breeze that comes through his nostrils and makes a sound.

"I know," he said, looking at me with his eyes traveling my face.

"You got a glass of ice cold milk in there too?" I asked jokingly, leaning to peek into the basket.

"Yep."

I was stunned, because he really did have milk, cold milk

and a box of Boston Baked Beans for dessert. Where he found them I have no idea because I didn't even know they still made the things. We ate in silence, just looking at each other. I've been wined and dined at some of the fanciest places, shimmed at some exotic resorts, but I don't remember it ever feeling this romantic.

"Thank you Grant," I finally said. I was surprised he remembered the things I liked and told him so.

He laughed. "Woman, who can forget, you ate those things like they were going out of style. Besides, I wanted to do something to help you recapture that innocence.

"It did."

I meant that too. It felt so good just to feel that good. Just to be myself not trying to prove anything. The wind was blowing my hair out of place and I didn't care. My clothes were wrinkling under me and I didn't care. I feel free…alive.

"Come here," Grant said.

I eased into his arms, just rested my back up against his chest. His arms folded around me like a blanket. We just sat there watching the birds and squirrels play. Our spirits had the sweetest conversation and neither of us said a word. Every so often I could feel Grant take a deep breath. I leaned my head back so I could see his face. He looked down at me and asked, "What you thinking about?"

"Nothing and everything. I just wanted to look at you."

"You can look as long as you'd like."

And that's what I did until it was time for me to go back to work. I photographed every inch of his face into my memory.

Grant and I decided to cook dinner together. Nothing fancy, keeping it simple like we did at lunch; hamburgers, french fries and my pecan pie. I've eaten more bread today than I have in the past month. I don't like to eat a lot. If you ever heard a camera adds pounds, believe it. So, in order for me to look like a size six on the air, I have to maintain a size four, so I don't eat.

Mitch says that's too small for someone my height and that a man likes meat on his bones. Grant hasn't said anything though I suspect he probably agrees with Mitch and would like to feel a little more body in his arms. Which is where I am now, feels like I'm supposed to be in them and he's in no hurry to push me away.

"Are you happy Malena Dawson?"

"Right now, yes."

"No, in general, are you happy?"

I moved out of his arms and he followed me into the living room where we sat in front of the fireplace.

"Are you happy Grant Carpenter?"

He smiled at me. "I'm extremely happy, and not just right now. So, answer my question woman."

"Yes, I'm happy *allllll* the time," I answered trying to contain a laugh.

Grant is funny even when he's trying not to be and it just tickles me.

"I worry about you."

"Don't. I'm fine, don't I look it?"

A passion flickered in his eyes before he answered.

"Yes, you look fine. You seem fine."

"But?"

"There is no but, I just want what's best for you."

"Let's change the subject, you're starting to sound like Momma and Mitch and I don't want this night to be ruined."

He took my hand into his and pulled me towards him.

"Malena, it's only because we love you that we care."

I tried to pretend like I didn't hear him say, "we love you" and I was too afraid to ask because I didn't want to get my feelings hurt.

"'We love you,' is that what you just said?"

Okay, I'm nosey and asked.

He cupped my hands in his face and his head just shook from side to side.

"Malena, I have always loved you and I always will. I

told you that."

"Yeah, when you were what, eight?"

"Ten, get it right, " he laughed. "But have I not shown it to you all these years?"

"You used to, but you stopped."

"What!" he said pulling away from me. "You're joking, right?"

"Does it look like I'm joking?" I asked. I knew I should have brought Valerie up, instead I let it stew and this was coming out wrong.

"Grant, again, at one point I was secure in what you said, but you stopped."

"No, you stopped. You needed a challenge and I didn't have time to give you one," he said calmly but with firmness to his tone.

The evening is not turning out the way I thought because Grant's forehead has more lines than a sheet of paper and I think I've got him beat.

"I wasn't looking for a challenge Grant, you tell me all this stuff, get my hopes up and then what did you do, moved on with Valerie."

"I didn't move on with anyone, and how do you know about Valerie?"

"Because she kindly told me when I called you one night that she was your lady and she'd appreciate it if I left you alone."

"Why didn't you call back, Malena?" he asked, ignoring my statement.

"I couldn't."

Grant's voice raised and deepened. "Couldn't? You couldn't? You pick up the phone and say, "Hey Grant, it's me."

"I wasn't about to chase behind you."

"Now, I know. I don't believe you. You based an entire lifetime on one call."

"What would you have done?"

"I would have trusted you," he said raising his voice a notch, "I would have trusted you and called back until I heard those words from your mouth."

"You didn't bother to correct it either, Grant."

"I tried. I called you and got your answering machine over and over. But it was easier for you to believe a stranger you didn't know than to trust me. Thanks Malena."

This conversation is going from bad to worse. And tears are trying very hard to push themselves past my lids. I stood up and walked off.

"Don't you walk away from me Malena."

I kept walking until I felt myself being pulled into his arms. Grant's right hand gently went around the back of my neck and he pressed his face to mine until they touched. In a voice filled with passion, desire, want, need and love, he said.

"Don't ever, I mean *ever*, doubt me or my feelings for you, Malena Dawson. I love you, I love you, I love, you," he continued to say until his mouth found mine. That man kissed me in a way that must have moved heaven. Kissed me like he knew me.

Not Interested

I couldn't believe of all the job offers I received, one was back in Biloxi, Mississippi. I began to get a little bored at work and the format on the show had changed so much it was hard to tell what we were doing from one day to the next. One day I arrived at work and there was a message from Milton Barrass. I was familiar with his name, he used to be the news director at one of the major networks in Washington, but for whatever reason he'd taken a position at my little old hometown station WGLL-TV. I was kind enough to return his call to let him know I wasn't interested. I thanked him for the opportunity and told him one day I might possibly reconsider.

I have to admit I was shocked by what they were willing to pay me. I would have been making a considerable amount more than I was already making and some other places I had applied, in addition to having a say in the direction I wanted to take the show. He had my attention for a minute until he said it was hosting a Christian program. My body tensed up. I was the last person that needed to host a Christian program. But for whatever reason Milton was convinced that I was the right person for the job and said he'd make the offer again and soon.

Grant thought it was a wonderful opportunity for me, which was a bit baffling to me considering he knew my past, but I didn't say anything. He'd managed three trips to Atlanta in a little over a month and time was too precious for unnecessary debates. Although we were tempted, there were a few times we thought of not telling Mitch he was in town but felt guilty about it. But, Mitch being Mitch, spent about thirty minutes with us then left saying he had to do some things for Stacy while he was giving Grant, that 'I've got your back man', look.

Grant and I spent most of our time together, just being together, in each others arms, talking, listening, sharing and caring. He knew things I didn't mention, felt things I never spoke. It was scary at times the spiritual connection that coursed between us, but we were both happily rooted. We shared the same bed when he visited but that was all we shared.

I knew when I got involved with him that sex would not be a part of this relationship. It felt good to give my all to a man, without giving him everything.

There was one moment of weakness his first visit. I walked out into the living room in my robe to get my purse. Grant was sitting on the couch with his eyes closed. My body must have shot up to nuclear status that day. He looked so sexy to me, so handsome. I turned to walk back to my bedroom and ended up walking to sit down next to him. Neither one of us said a word, I wouldn't call it lust that we were feeling, but something behind my heart drew me into his arms. He kissed me in a way that hurt, it was so sensual and passionate. One of his hands was stroking my face, while the other was loosening the tie on my robe. His hands felt like fire when it touched my exposed breast. As bad as we both wanted it, we knew this was out of order. It took a few more strokes before we finally stopped. But that was probably the worst or best we've ever gotten to being out of line.

Many times, he just rests in my bosom and we talk. He says he feels comfortable in my chest, that Jesus rested in God's chest and I'm his second source of comfort. And that's how it is with us, lots of solitude, co-joining of the spirits and no sex. I know that's Grant's way of saying he trusts me enough to lie in my protection, though one day I'll actually be under his.

I thought I'd have trouble desiring him again but I haven't. I can't explain it to you, it's just a knowing between us now that can't be tampered with by indulging in sex. So we keep it sweet and pure. Sometimes with Grant, it's as if we are together bowed down on our knees in the presence of our Father in Heaven.

Pam, being Pam, asked if we had hit the sheets yet.

"No, and we won't."

"What? Why?"

"It's not like that with us Pam, it's special, there's a purity to this union."

"Oh, he a punk."

"PAM!"

"Calm down, girl, but I just ain't never heard of what you talking about. And he's young, but I have to admit the man is very easy on the eyes and I just find it hard believe."

"Well, it's not going to happen. We've discussed it, but I knew it before hand."

"Did you?"

"Yes. He told me he'd never uncover me, I was too special for that."

"Uncover? Girl, that man will be okay, it ain't that much Bible reading in the world."

"I didn't think you'd understand Pam," I said walking off.

I regretted telling Pam afterwards, it was hard to understand even for me at times. I know it's not rare to find a man who's waiting, but I haven't run across any. And there's something so kind about a man willing to wait for you, especially when the desire is so strong but his righteousness and respect for you means more. Yeah, I can see why Pam would have a problem with this. Prior to Grant, so would I.

I'm glad I didn't tell her he was a virgin, because a mind like Pam's couldn't comprehend that. I remember the night we discussed it. I was sitting in his lap on the couch with my head resting in his neck. I asked him if I could trust him? He didn't say anything, just leaned over and began reading to me an article on love that one of his friends had written for the church. He was focused as he read:

How many arrows must your heart endure before you realize you've fallen in love again? The kind of love based on roses, chocolates, romantic dinners and sexual escapades if you're so inclined. A love that in the beginning your significant other's words sound better than raindrops and glisten brighter than the stars above. The kind of love that ultimately brings you to a place of 'How did I get here?" Or worst yet, what was going on within me that I allowed this person to take time away from my life that I can never recover?

Grant stopped when I moved-that last line hit a nerve with me.

"Go ahead sweetie, finish."

The bigger question is why did it take a year to figure out what I knew in the first few weeks. I fell, not for the person but into emotional bondage. Real love is about growth, not necessarily in other people but within your own spirit. Yet, many of us chose to stay in a love that keeps us bound. A love that demands a return at the expense of our fledging spirit. Even God gives free will, a choice to love him. Love is trust that's not manipulated, a feeling that goes hand in hand with our innermost being.

Grant stopped in the middle of the article and inhaled deep within his nostrils. His chest was slowly rising and falling. His tone had changed, sounded like he was fighting back tears. I thought he was going to finish the article, instead he just said, "Malena, if you ever feel compelled to ask me again if you can trust me,, maybe we're moving too fast."

I didn't mean to offend him, but I knew I had and probably would have felt the same way had he'd asked me that question. I adjusted myself in his lap so I could see his face.

"I like our pace Grant, I do. I apologize for doubting you. I know there are things you know about me that I haven't shared, but I just feel like I need to tell you."

"Talk to me. There's nothing you can't share with me."

"Grant, I know you're a virgin, but I'm not--I think you know that," I said as a tear slipped.

I didn't realize how much it bothered me until I realized I had not waited for the real thing to come. I know men, or at least I've heard that men don't like to think about their woman being with anyone but them, so I was shocked by his response.

He closed his eyes and I knew he was praying about what I'd just revealed, then he said, "That's because I didn't have you first," and left our conversation and continued in prayer with our Father.

He pulled my head to his chest and I know you will think I'm crazy, but I could hear what they were saying, and it wa the most peaceful moment I've ever known.

.

Feels So Good

Love has made me lazy—in a good way of course. I've slowed down a little. Not enough-just a little. But when Grant's in town, you need a search party to locate me. We've shared an amazing three months together. I never thought about it until after he left that we'd have to maintain this relationship long distance, but it hasn't felt like that. We've managed to see each other three weekends out of the months sometimes lasting four days, plus the nightly calls and it's enough to sustain us both. Of course Grant still tells me, "Even when I'm not with you Malena, I'm with you--that's how it's always been."

That makes sense to me because I carry that man with me everywhere, too. Thinking about how he looks at me with his eyes. I remember the story of Mary Magdeline and how Jesus cleansed her making her pure with His words by saying, "Your sins have been forgiven." She wept at His feet and I can only imagine why, to have eyes look at you that see past the mess and behold your innocence. I'm not comparing Grant to Jesus. I'm not that in love, but Jesus definitely lives in him. For in his eyes, his voice and his embrace there is no judgment of my past behavior.

He's headed in tonight and I can't wait to see him although I just came back from visiting him a week ago for his parent's twenty-fifth wedding anniversary celebration. It felt more like a reunion, Mitch and his family, Momma and Sam and the two of us.

I didn't tell you. No one in our family was surprised to see we were a couple. The consensus has been all this time, "What took so long?" Seems a bet was made that I would have buckled before I did. I'm glad I didn't, not sure if I could have appreciated the man that he is, had I not endured the foolishness from my past. We actually discussed it after his parents' party. I flat out told him the things I had convinced myself I just had to have. I thought it would cause this huge debate but he actually looked at me like he felt sorry for me and said, "How long do you think money and status would have made you happily married to a man you didn't love, Malena?"

I had my plans so laid out I never really thought about it, just the present and what those relationships brought then, and I told him that on our drive back to his house.

"I'm surprised that you hadn't."

"Why is that?"

"Well, I never met your father, but I remember the stories you and Mitch shared with me and there were times I overheard your Momma talking about him with mine. I just thought you'd seen real and would want the same for yourself."

"That kind of love is rare, Grant. It's almost like setting yourself up to be hurt."

I was resting my hand behind his head massaging it with my fingertips. I felt him tense up after that comment.

"Malena, if you feel that way, what are we doing here?"

I turned to look at him. His eyes were focused on the highway.

"Grant, you understand what I mean, don't you?"

"Not really."

"Well, the love my parents shared and the love your parents share—love is just not like that anymore. It's based on other things, don't you think?"

"Amazing. You almost sound as if you've convinced yourself that you believe that. Malena, love has no face."

"Come on Grant, be honest. We have more to choose from than our parents did. Folks aren't settling now."

"So, you think our parents settled?"

"That's not what I'm saying Grant and you know that."

"Do I? I mean it sounds like 'your' idea of love is based on something else and I need to know."

He had a concern on his face, one I had no intentions of causing.

"Grant," I said rubbing the side of his face, "I love you, but I know that not everyone has a chance to feel this. I never said what we had wasn't rare. It's just most people don't wait long enough to find this."

Grant looked at me with this smile playing across his mouth. He rubbed his hands over his mouth and said, "Do you realize what you just said?"

"Yeah, that our love is rare. I believe that."

"No, you just said you loved me, Malena."

"And?"

"That's the first time you've said that in all this time."

He was right, but it was hard to believe that was the first time. I loved him so much and had for sometime. I guess I just felt it so strong, it was like it had already been spoken. That night was somewhat a turning point for us, in a good and in a bad way, but I wouldn't realize that until later.

What Has Happened Here?

Grant and I are celebrating our four month anniversary this weekend. Yes, we're counting months. I look at him sometimes and still can't believe he exists or how or why God chose to bless me with him. Grant insists that God revealed to him all those years ago that the two of us would be together. I've learned that when he talks about God not to question it. I've never seen someone as passionate about the Lord as he is. He goes someplace else when he speaks of God, even when he's in the same room. I can always tell when he's in deep thought with God, his skin is almost illuminated, there's this inward glow that just draws you to him. He's just wonderful.

I know you may be tired of hearing that, but he is. It finally feels right, you know, right--like I'm supposed to be here. His method of lovemaking is so sweet the way he strokes my mind and embraces my soul. He's wonderful or I'm just in love, probably a little of both. Anyway, Grant says that he has always known that we would be together. And, I never associated 'together' with 'forever'. Until he produced a two carat engagement ring and asked me to marry him.

I saw a look of concern on his face when I didn't answer

immediately. The fact is, I couldn't. I loved Grant, there was no doubt at all about that. I wanted to share my life with him, but marriage had never entered my mind. As I looked at him on his knees, waiting for an answer my heart tied itself into knots.

"I know you're nervous baby," Grant said with a half smile.

"Grant, I..."

"What is it Malena?"

I honestly felt like I was about to pass out. I kept seeing in my head my family, me and Grant married, him leaving me behind with kids and me suffering in silent agony as Momma had done all those years. I knew I couldn't marry him-that would be like losing him. My mind wouldn't let me see it any other way.

"Grant, I can't marry you," I said through tears.

"WHAT?"

Grant stood up and glared at me. I couldn't even look up into his eyes. I didn't want to see the pain I knew I had put there. If he yelled that would help, but he didn't. If he'd breathed heavy that would help, but he didn't. He just stood there looking at me as if he'd just laid eyes on me for the first time.

"Grant, let me explain...try to at least."

He threw his hands up in the air and just shook his head in unbelief and said, "Spare me Malena, please."

"I love you Grant, I honestly love you."

"Malena. Sweet Malena. I don't think you know what true love is baby. And, you know what? I'm tired, I'm just too tired to do this with you anymore."

Grant left that night and disappeared as if he'd never known me. I kept thinking he'd cool down and eventually call and he never did. He didn't accept my calls, sent my letters back unopened, it was like he'd never known me. If it weren't for Mitch and Momma I wouldn't know if he were okay or not. Mitch told me one night over dinner to give him time because he was hurting.

"Well, I'm hurt too, Mitch."

"Malena, its different,. And you have to be fair."

"Mitch, I loved that man and you know it."

"Malena, you're my sister. I love you, but you say that, and it's hard to believe with your actions sometimes. Grant has been so patient with you all these years. Even these last four months, you've taken that poor man through a few trials with that job and your running."

"I have not been running Mitch, but I do have a career."

"And you think Grant doesn't. Do you even know what he's working on Malena? I'm willing to bet his responsibilities are larger than yours, but he's the one always coming to you. He's always there for you, always has been."

"Mitch, you sound like you're upset with me."

"Malena, I just don't get you sometimes. Like I said, I love you, but you've changed so much over the years. It was great to see your beauty again when Grant came back into your life. That light was lit inside you again. But I'm curious, what the heck are you hiding behind?"

"Grant walked out my life, but all this is my fault? I don't believe you Mitch."

"He loved you sis."

"And I loved him, he knows that."

"Malena, again, you say that, but you've never given that man reason to truly trust in it. And he put his heart on the line when he proposed."

Mitch had me with that, I couldn't argue. I had become so used to Grant being there for me that I didn't realize how little I was there for him, but he never said a thing, not once. And now he was out of my life. But I wasn't giving up, I intended to fight and I did just that until I received a letter from him six months later that clearly let me know he was done with me.

Letter to Malena Dawson

Our love was incomplete. A word was missing. The word: you. It never had anything to do with I or You, it was about the love in the middle. God is love darling. Not career, ambition, selfishness, but God. Our love ended with a question mark. I Love; I love what? Or was it love you; love what? It ended without I or You on either side of God. You were a treasure to me. Someone who made me open and receptive to love. But you threw it away and for what? Fear?

Or a career that leaves you unfulfilled and rocks you to sleep at night? I wonder if one day what you gain will be worth what you've lost. You were so accustomed to receiving my love that you took it for granted. Did you not realize that I had a life too? Dreams just like you that I hoped we'd share together one day? Did you ever wonder how my day went?

Did you ever think your shoulder was needed to catch my tears at times, like mine caught yours so often? The desire to partake in that joyous wonder that is love with you cost me. I yielded to you and entered into a place of disobedience. I can tell you now, what I lost, no amount of wealth can reclaim. You took my love and cast it out into this desolate world. As much as

I want to hate you now, my spirit won't let me, my spirit that connected with yours so many memories ago. Your conscience may be satisfied now that your decision was based on some convoluted analogy you created in your head. But, sweet Malena, your spirit will never know peace until love is complete. I will end this now knowing in my heart that you were treated kindly. With love, respect, and honor; treated like the royal princess that is you. As God is my witness, I will find the treasure I deserve in my life, and live with the knowledge that love is incomplete because a word is missing-you. I wish you the best in life, but it's time we end the pain. I pray that you will find all that you have searched for that you were unable to find in me.

With Love,
Grant

I read that letter and it broke my heart. Grant was wrong, off base. He was good enough for me. He was right for me. I was the problem. I WAS THE PROBLEM! I feel if I say it loud enough and often enough he'll somehow hear me. But so much time has passed.

I read his letter everyday, even though my tears have faded the ink on the recycled paper-it's memorized in my heart. I can still see where he crossed his "T"s and dotted his "I"s and the stains from where his tears must have fallen as he drafted that letter. Touching this letter is like touching him. It's all I have left of him besides my memories. And I don't have a right to have those since he's moved on. Does it bother me that he

didn't fight for me? Yes! It hurts too because he was right. But I can't blame him if he hates me the rest of his life. I hate myself right now. I fought tooth and nail for everything else, for my chance in the spotlight, position, power, but didn't have the endurance to fight for the greatest love I know I'll ever know. I should have been more focused on lighting a glow within me-but it wasn't bright enough, not for a man like Grant. He was four years younger and possessed more wisdom than anyone I've ever known. See, it wasn't him.

There I go again, repeating myself, but that happens when you start to realize the mistakes you've made. I found that light I wanted so bad and have the burn marks to prove it. Was it worth everything I gave up. No! None of it was worth it. Yet here I am a few breaths away from turning twenty-seven, more lost than I was at eight the day I saw my Daddy in that box almost twenty years ago. I know one thing, I'm a selfish woman because I was trying to get Grant back, not because he needed me, but because I needed him. He was right, I was so busy basking in the glow of his love that I never really showed him how special he was to me. I knew he would be okay though. I knew that this would only push him closer to God and there was peace for me because I knew he was hurting and if God had him dwelling in his secret place, he would be okay. If you can hear me Grant Carpenter, I really do love you.

Change of Plans

Remember how Billie Holiday, Sarah Vaughn and Sam Cooke used to sing. They didn't sing to impress, just sang from the heart and somehow their pain came out sounding like heaven's angels. Right now I'm STILL singing to impress and I sound like a scratched record played backwards.

"You coming home for Thanksgiving?" Momma asked, "I think the trip will do you good."

"I'm going to try Momma, so much is going on here."

"I know and that's why you need to be around family. You need a vacation"

"I know," was all I said.

Momma was right but I was still having a hard time being around her and Sam. After all those years, they married. Samuel Waters has taken Daddy's place. He's a good man and I know he makes Momma smile real nice, but seeing him at our table takes me back too many years ago to another face that use to occupy our table. And I can't even talk about Grant. It hurts too bad. It's been three hundred and sixty-five days of sheer pain without him in my life.

"Malena, I know what the problem is, and sweetie, you

will have to accept Sam eventually."

"I like him Momma, you know that. I always have."

"Liking someone and accepting them Malena is two different things."

"Momma what are you talking about?"

"I'm going to say this and then I'm hanging up this phone," she said sternly. "To be yourself and accepted is love manifested into reality, don't you ever forget that," and hung up the phone.

Momma's message was loud and clear. Too loud. Trying to get past Grant landed me in deeper junk than ever before. I'm seeing someone else again. He fits the profile—fine, educated, older, successful attorney. He's here now. We just finished ruffling my sheets. Yes, I'm back to ruffling these filthy sheets after being around something so pure.

And you know what, it still doesn't feel right and hasn't felt right with any man, but Grant and he never touched me. So my life went backwards instead of moving forward. I thought it was crazy before, but it's insane now. It's so phony now to still be living this kind of life. Even Pam is still the same, but wilder if that's possible. Partying like it's going to stop any day and a new boyfriend every other week. She was promoted to account director. That girl has always been good with numbers. I guess she has to be to count all her men.

Let me stop, I don't want to shine the light on her, because I'm still trying to fix my own. I'm trying again, going to church to get a word, but I'm not hearing anything and there's an emptiness inside of me that I can't explain. I feel like I've not only let myself, my family, and Grant down, but now I feel like I let the Lord down. I have it all--the career, the home and the man.

Oh, let me tell you about this man. Kenneth is fine and loaded like I used to want, but he has a temper out of this world. He hasn't hit me yet, but sometimes his eyes tells me he wants too. I think the only reason he hasn't is because he knows I'll hurt his yellow butt when he goes to sleep. Yes, he's light, just like I used to want and with curly hair too. But as evil and selfish as the day is light. Kenneth honestly believes this world revolves around him. I mean honestly. His schedule is the same as mine, but he expects and doesn't give. I don't think this man once in an entire year has asked me how my day was and he only asks about my family when I bring them up. And will go off in a minute if you disagree with him.

Interesting how I called him over here tonight to break it off and I let him talk me out of it. I think he knew what was on my mind when I called him, which is why he came over here with roses and strawberries hanging from his tongue.

That's not why I changed my mind though. I can't tell you why but I know I should have gone through with it. Because I'm looking down at him and occupying my bed I see a stranger that I don't like. I can't stand him, if you want to know the truth. So, who has the real problem? Me, right? But I used to want this lifestyle but it never was fulfilling and it's still not. Lots of fancy functions, hanging with the elite, but at the end of the day I feel like I've been acting. I talked to Pam about it. We share everything still, except our men, that's one area we DO NOT cross. But she thinks I'm not giving Kenneth a fair chance. We talked about it one Saturday afternoon.

"Girl, have you lost your mind? Do you know how many women would kill for that brother?" she said after I told her I wanted to end things with him.

"Pam, it's not real, we're just going through the motions."

"Who gives a flip about some motions," she said standing up to cut a piece of pecan pie (Mrs. Mables recipe) I'd made earlier. "He's got money, is fine and I know he makes you scream, I heard you across town."

I laughed but didn't mean it. Pam didn't hold back anything.

"Girl, you nasty and you ain't heard nobody screaming."

"Girl, I almost called the police when that brother first started coming over here it was so loud."

"See, now you just lying."

We both had to laugh then.

"Seriously, Pam, don't you ever get tired?"

"Of what? Girl, I'm having too much fun."

"That's what I mean, fun. Neither one of us is over the hill, but it's starting to feel like too much is missing."

Pam took a big piece of pie in her mouth and mumbled, "Girl, I will change when I'm ready to change and not a minute before then. I just think you and Kenneth need to get away for a little while so you can get back on track."

I shook my head.

"I'm on track Pam, that's the thing. I kept remembering that article Grant read to me about wasting time with the wrong person. It took me a year to realize what I knew in three weeks, he's not for me."

"Well, who is? Let me guess."

"Pam, it's not anyone, it's me, it's about my walk with the Lord and finally knowing what I want."

"It's Grant. I know it's Grant."

"It's not Grant. It's the Lord, Pam, the Lord and growing closer to his leading. I mean are you really happy, I mean *really* happy?"

"Shoot yeah."

"See, I'm not. And, I'm not going to find it in a man, including Grant, it's not in that job, it's deep inside of me and I don't know who 'me' is anymore and I need to reconnect with my inner man."

"Malena, you tripping now girl."

"Maybe I am, but I doubt it. I just wonder why I think I have to wait until I'm sixty to give my life to Jesus. That's what's missing from my life and not feeling Him is scary."

"Girl, please don't tell me all this is over that little boy," she said as if she hadn't heard a word I said.

"Pam, you've got one more time and I do mean one, to say something negative about Grant," I said.

She never said another word, nor did she change her mind. I think partly because we had a pact. This was the way we planned to live and in some ways if I changed I'd be leaving her behind. I guess that's a possibility because I just can't see continuing in this lie I call life. Especially when I see years passing by that I can't get back. And I'm not eight anymore. I know what fruit is now and Kenneth's is rotten when you get to the core and mine ain't the best when I'm around him. But that's about to change right now.

I shook him lightly at first.

"Kenneth, wake up, we need to talk."

"Not now Malena," he said twisting his body from my hand.

I shook harder.

"Kenneth, wake up, I said we need to talk."

"And I said, not now Malena," he said burying his head into the pillow.

I shook even harder.

"Wake up, we need to talk."

He rolled over, raised up and faced me. I knew that moment I'd been sharing my bed with the enemy from the look on his face. Fear gripped my heart and flipped it backwards. I didn't have enough anointing in my life to cast off a cold, let alone the devil.

The Altar

The dreams began again after all the years. The voice of the angel reading to me in my dreams. I woke up in tears, sobbing, pleading and asking God for forgiveness for all the sins I'd committed against Him. I was begging in a way I didn't know existed within me. As I cried it really hit, that's what had been missing all this time–the Lord. I tried to replace Him with everything and came up short. There is no comparison. I realized that I had grown so far from Him that I felt ashamed and guilty to even ask that He receive me again.

To make matters worse, when I pulled closer to Him and felt his presence, I'd walk away as soon as the next best thing, career or whatever, came along. I was out there in the world. I was unstable in the Lord and the more time went past the more empty I felt inside. I was so weak in my faith that I couldn't see that God's Word speaks truth. I know now, I want the blood, the blood in my life, the word I was raised on, the peace I knew as a child. I want it back. I always felt I'd get it right when I got older like you see most people in the church. But God didn't plan to let me wait that long and I didn't want to anymore. I knew in my heart that He had, not because God has to, because

His Word says He will. I let the enemy take the fear from my past and mutilate my future. I could have had a new talk show that offered something positive, a great love ordained by God and I chose to live in denial. But, God is forgiving, merciful and His love will endure.

I know now that voice telling me "Daughter of mine, go forth" was the voice of God. As I remember that, I feel an overwhelming sense of peace, that evil can't manipulate. Even being with Grant, as much as I loved him (and always will) there was only so much he could do. But that night the angel came I made up my mind finally, that if I was going to suffer in life it would be for Christ. I knew after Kenneth there was no way I could continue in those empty relationships anymore, and I didn't want too. Plus, I knew that time would have to pass before I could allow someone in my heart again, because Grant still pretty much owned it.

The day after the dream I went to church. It was like I was running to Jesus. I went down on the altar, confessed and repented for every offense I could think of and ones I didn't remember. With each confession a weight was lifted off my chest. I felt the presence of the Holy Spirit embracing and delivering me and I knew at that moment I'd never be the same again. That's what I had been running from all those years–the Truth.

And if you can believe it, I'm moving back to Biloxi. That job Milton Barras offered me is still available. I'm excited about it. It's new, but there's a peace in this decision and I'll learn as I go. I've let go all those foolish and silly ideas I have of what success and confidence means. True confidence, I've learned, is being yourself, letting your guard down and admitting you are human and flawed. Success is found in the center of our hearts when we fill it with compassion. So I knew I would be okay. A new job, a new beginning back in my hometown. My life felt whole after that and I had faith that God would do what He needed to in my life. My trust was in Him when I turned in my resignation, and gave them a month notice. Well, someone in the powers that be must have been upset, because they piled even more work on me. In fact, gave me other peoples' work. Even though I found spiritual healing, all the years of wear and tear on my physical and emotional body was about to catch up to me.

Lights, Camera...Burnout

Though I was in a different place spiritually, the last month had worn me out to the point of exhaustion. My schedule was hectic before and I've added things on top of things trying to get ready to move. The move. The only thing to give me peace of mind in the midst of the chaos. If I kept going I didn't have to think about all the new things about to happen. After receiving Grant's letter, I tried to contact him a few more times and he still refused to talk with me. This was definitely not another misunderstanding like before with Valerie, which he did explain to me. These were words from his mouth. He was still kind, but it seemed that he had purged himself of me.

In all the years I'd known Grant, I never thought there would come a day when he'd not be there for me, but he wasn't. I needed him, but it had also come to a point where I knew I needed Jesus more. I was playing hide and go seek Christian for too long and if I knew Grant, he was doing exactly what he was being led by the Spirit to do, which was probably to stay away from me. The emptiness inside of me was evident and Grant could only do so much, and this was so much more than that.

Grant loves me too much to let me put him above the

Lord or the calling He's placed in my life. So I just pray about it and him. In fact, I was praying to myself when Mario, my cameraman and I had arrived at the abortion clinic where I was doing a three-part segment on legal and theological perspective son abortion. I knew when I stepped inside the clinic that morning that things were about to change in another way spiritually for me.

This place was familiar–too familiar. No, I never had an abortion, but I had become so adamant about not having children that somewhere in the back of my mind this could have one day been an option. We were waiting on the administrator to get off a conference call so I decided to look around. I was flipping through a personal profile they give to their patients to complete; a standard form asking last, first and middle name, etcetera. All of a sudden, I felt like writing "coward" on it. That's how I had being living my life, in utter fear, planning things out to the point of obsession. I had planned my life right into a wall.

"Did you hear that?" I asked Mario.

"Hear what?"

"It sounds like a baby crying," I said looking around.

"Malena, I'm not trying to be funny, but we are in an abortion clinic. I doubt you hear a baby."

He had a point but I could hear a baby crying. Mario was too nice to say he thought I was losing it. But I heard what I heard. The crying finally stopped.

"I hear you were offered a job in Biloxi, hosting your own Christian talk show."

"How did you know about that?"

"Walter."

"How did he know? I never said anything to him. Never mind, don't answer," I said with somewhat of an attitude.

"Malena, are you okay this morning? You seem sort of edgy."

"Yeah, fine," I said and stood up to walk around.

"I tell you what, while we wait, let me get some visual aid shots of you."

"Okay.".

Mario flipped the light on the camera and positioned it in front of me. When the light hit my eyes I heard the sounds of babies again. The crying grew louder piercing through my ears to my heart. "What is that noise?" I asked him again.

"I don't hear anything Malena," Mario said.

I tried to smile, but my lip refused to curl into the smile befitting a talk show host. I looked around. The walls began spinning. The crying, the crying. It was the sound of every soul that was lost inside a plastic bag tossed out into a bin marked "hazardous" at the end of the day. It was the sound of life, hope, missed childhoods, dying at the hands of a stranger in a white coat and powdered gloves. All of a sudden, I could hear what my Daddy said about Sardines.

You should never take a child away from its mother, even if it's just a fish.

"Daddy."

"Malena, are you alright?" Mario asked lowering the camera down by his side and walking up to me.

I could see him, feel his touch, but I couldn't hear him, just the sounds growing louder. I still heard cries of baby booties and wide-eyed innocent, ponytails tied back with colorful ribbons and bows.

Never take a child away from its parent, even if it's just a fish...never steal God's time.

"Help me God, please help me," I said out loud.

Daughter of mine, go forth.

Tears swelled up inside of me, this was the sound of God crying for the mothers that didn't trust him enough to bring them through the birth of a miracle. It wasn't about a baby, it was about life, the life He has given us as a gift that we often chose to ruin by disobedience and fear. The life He had given me was real, planted by a seed of love, tenderness and adoration. And on top of that, He had gifted me with the same kind of love of my own, a union formed by spirit and not flesh.

Never take a child away from its parent, even if it's just a fish. Never take a child away from its parent, even if it's just a fish. Never take a child away from its parent, even if it's just a fish.

I thought I'd cried before but it felt like something heavy hit me in the back and knocked me to my knees and opened a floodgate. I started crying so violently (more like screaming) my body hurt. Like something had a hold of me in the gut tightening its hold on me, birthing me. I could see Mario looking at me, not knowing what to do...I heard myself screaming my Daddy's name, crying for all those years I never said bye, crying for all the memories I stifled to keep from remembering him. I cried for being so disobedient, rebellious, but I knew in those tears that God's mercy endured. I rolled into a ball and just felt myself rocked in the presence of the Holy Spirit unlike ever before. I knew for certain then I was renewed. This one stunt could have cost me my career and I didn't care. I continued to cry to the Lord and at the moment, nothing else mattered but the LORD! No career, no money, no fame-just the LORD!

Pray for Her

The sound of something falling woke me from my sleep. I woke up, looked around the room and couldn't figure out what it was. My heart was racing inside my chest and I just felt lost for a moment. I knew whatever I was feeling was connected to Malena. She was three hours ahead of me so I knew she was at work. I got up and walked to the telephone to call the airlines. I didn't know what was wrong but I knew she needed me. Something took hold of me and brought me to my knees as I begin to pray for her.

Father God, I thank you, I thank you for your presence in my life. Father, I ask that you santicfy my heart, mind and spirit. Thank you Jesus. Father I just want to usher Malena Dawson into your embrace right now at this very moment. My heart and spirit is troubled for her and I can feel in me that she needs you. I ask that you touch her with your grace, mercy and love Dear Lord. I ask that your countenance come upon her right now Father and give her peace in her mind and spirit. Protect her, Dear Lord, until such time that you entrust her with me again. I give thanks to you in all things Father. I give thanks to you for her healing according to your word. Lord, let it be done according to your will, not mine, but your will be done. In Jesus name, Amen.

I feel a little better now that I've prayed and decided to wait and call her later. This past year has been somewhat torture for me, but also a period of growth. I said some things to Malena I shouldn't have. I made up my mind that I was done with her, but that's not what God wanted me to do and I knew it. He was working in me with her, teaching me about His love. And, part of loving her was letting her go to find herself. She couldn't do it in my presence. It was like I was stifling her. So, it's been a period of submission for me waiting on the Lord to give me the okay to find her again. That time had come, this peace came over me and I've never heard my Father speak as clear as he did today.

"Son, she's ready...go and get your wife."

I didn't even pack, just threw on some jeans and a sweatshirt and drove straight to the airport. I'll worry about clothes when I get there. My baby needs me and is ready for me—I can feel it and I know it.

Wake Up Princess!

I wasn't sure where I was when I opened my eyes. My head felt heavy and my body was a little achy, but I'd never felt better in my life. My eyes landed on stuffed teddy bears piled in the corner and I thought I was in my old room for a second. I was at my house, but someone had brought some of my old things to surround me. Just then Momma peeked her head in the room and I felt like I was ten years old again.

"Hi Princess," she whispered.

I smiled at her. She hadn't called me that in years, even in private. She made me feel like a little girl and from the look in her eyes I guess I always would be her baby.

"What are you doing here?"

"You know I had to come check on you. You scared us."

After the emotional cry at the clinic, Mario drove me home and called Mitch for me. He arrived in record time and I just remember holding onto him and crying and saying, "I'm fine, I'm free Mitch. I'm free."

I think Mitch knew what was happening though I didn't go into detail, because he started crying with me and held me like he did so many years ago outside of our parents' bedroom when we thought our Daddy had come home. He was protecting me. Always had been really. I just wouldn't receive the love that was so freely given to me. I chose to keep it at somewhat of a distance.

"I feel rested," I said sitting up straight, "and good."

"You've been sleeping the past twenty-four hours. You look refreshed," she said smiling at me.

"I'm sorry Momma."

"What's wrong baby?" she asked grabbing my hand.

I was moved to tears. I was so ashamed of past behavior. I was so busy trying not to repeat the steps my mother made, that I never looked at how much she accomplished. My mother was a woman of grace, perservance and strength. Never once was she ashamed of what she had to endure to ensure our well-being. I never thought I was ashamed of her until I spent my entire life trying to be anything but her. Somewhere in college, the past and all that I'd lost was too much. I started seeing myself as my mother, married with children and then when it hit me that I could have that and lose Grant, that was too much to bear. The relationship Grant and I shared was so similar to that of my parents and his parents. I couldn't picture a life of loving him. The only thing I could see in my mind was losing him and I couldn't live with that. I could live with not being with him, knowing he was alive somewhere. So, when he proposed, my heart said yes, but my mind was fearful of the future. All of that fumbled from my mouth to my mother's ears. She never let go of my hand.

"I never knew you were ashamed of me, Malena."

It hurt my ears to hear the sadness that tipped my mother's tongue.

"Momma, I'm sorry, it was never about you. This was never about you."

"Baby, I know we didn't have much those earlier years but you never lacked loved, neither you or your brother."

"I know Momma, and that meant more than any amount of money I can make. But you know I never took the time to deal with Daddy's death. After all these years I've never once said bye to him in my heart until yesterday."

"I had no idea you hadn't let go."

"I couldn't. For so long I thought he was coming home and even when I was old enough to realize he wasn't, it was easier to pretend that I didn't remember him than to deal with knowing that I had and he really was gone."

"You talked about your Daddy often."

"Not really Momma. Think about it. I always found a reason to leave the room or changed the subject."

Momma lowered her head and a tear slipped from her face.

"I never realized that until just now Malena. I was in so much pain the first few years. I'm so sorry I never took the time to be there for you."

"Momma, that's just it, you were there. That's what I'm saying, I used you as an excuse to create all these superficial ideas in my head. The truth is I've been so afraid of finding a man like Daddy, having a family and then it being uprooted. At least by having a successful career, if something happened, I could take care of us, but then, he..."

"You grew in love with Grant?" Momma said with pride.

"Yes."

"Loving him reminded you of your father," she said more as a statement.

"Yes, I guess he always did and even when he was old enough, that still held me back. His wisdom, gentleness, kindness and I remember what Mrs. Mable said about Daddy showing me what to look for in a 'Godly' man."

"I remember her saying that," she said with a hint of nostaglia. "I'll tell you this baby, I don't know, can't understand what all you've been through. But, I tell you, loving your father was so great. I would have rather had one year with Mitchell than sixty with someone I didn't love."

"Momma you were so unhappy without him."

"Baby, yes, that was a mighty powerful love, but it was a love that was so strong it sustained me sixteen years. It's the kind of love I just couldn't settle for anything else. I'm grateful for the years I had with your father. Grateful honey. And remember you can't predict the future, so you can't assume that will happen with Grant. He loves you, he's a man of God and no matter what happens, you two are lifted before Him."

"I don't know that Grant would take me back and to be honest he deserves better than what I offered him. I hurt him trying to shield him from myself."

"He deserves what he wants and what God wants for him and that happens to be you."

"It used to be me, Momma. He's moved on with his life."

"Sounds like he still loves you to me."

"He called?" I asked calmly, though my heart was racing.

"Something like that, he flew down here, sensing that something was wrong with you. He was here earlier. He's over at Mitch's right now."

I didn't say anything to Momma. But while I slept I thought I'd felt his presence in my room. Initially, I thought I was crazy it was so strong. I also thought I heard him praying over me and rubbing my face and I had. He was here.

"I didn't think he'd ever speak to me again."

"Baby, that man loves you. Loves you in the right way in a way that he can't loose by himself."

"I think I finally understand that Momma. It reminds me of a scripture Daddy always quoted, 'Unless the Lord builds this house...'"

"They labor in vain who build it," Momma finished with a smile.

It felt like overnight all the lessons I was taught as a child make sense to me now. I've been trying to create my own destiny instead of yielding to the one given to me by God and trusting in it, that whether Grant and I have ten years or seventy, it's God's will, not ours and being obedient yields many blessings. I was trying to build houses that didn't belong to me instead of entering into the one he pre-ordained, Grant.

"Where are you going?" I asked Momma when she stood to leave.

"I'm going to call a man that's been waiting a long, very

long time for you."

I blushed, something I do in his presence and at the mere thought of him.

I've been waiting along time for him too and pray that its not too late.

Momma spoke with pride.

"It's not to late Princess, you two are right on time."

Wake Up Pineapple!

I felt his hands on my face. I purposely kept my eyes closed so he'd think I was still sleeping so I could feel the gentleness of his touch. My eyes fluttered open and I wanted to cry. All the love I knew he had for me was still in his eyes. Concern was in his eyes. I was in his eyes. He didn't, we didn't say anything, just looked at each other.

I finally spoke, or tried too.

"Grant, I'm sorry."

He placed his finger over my lips and shook his head.

"No apologies. That's behind us."

"Us? There's still an us?" I asked.

"You tell me. But we can't look back, Malena. God is telling me to say to you right now, 'Daughter, go forth'. I don't know what that means to you baby, but for me it means a new day."

Any other time my guard may have gone up, but I knew at that moment that risking love, life and the uncertainty of it all was worth it. Plus, my mind wrapped itself around his last three words, 'daughter, go forth'--confirmation from the Lord that he was it, part of my destiny. A secret no one knew but my Father in heaven and myself. I never told anyone about that and God had revealed it to him.

"There's still an us. It's always been us."

He leaned down and kissed me softly on my lips and then lifted me up into his arms and whispered in my ear. "I've missed you."

I thought my inside would explode with joy as I looked into his eyes and said, "Even when I'm not with you, I'm with you Grant," reminding him of what he's always told me. He just smiled that disarming grin that I knew would keep me on my toes forever and kissed me again.

I cleared my throat, mustered up a bit of boldness and said, "Give me my ring please."

Grant's head flew back in laughter.

"What makes you think I still have that ring? Or better yet, have it on me?"

"Because I know you," I said snuggling my face under his chin.

"And what if you're wrong?"

"Oh, I'm not."

"You're cocky, Malena Dawson."

"Nawww, I just know if you're here it's because you couldn't let go either. And I know if you're here now it's because it's our time. You once said that we can run from the flesh, but not from the spirit."

"I'm surprised you remember that. That was years ago."

"Grant Carpenter, there's nothing about you that escapes me, I'm just ready to receive and embrace it."

He inhaled and let out a deep breath through his nostrils. He slid his hands into his pants pocket and pulled out the ring box. He didn't ask me to marry him again; just slid the ring on my finger. We looked at each other and said at the same time, "Yes."

There was a calmness surrounding us, the presence of God shining down on His handiwork because this was truly one house God had built and one that would endure now that the fight was over. I felt it in my spirit and saw confirmation in his eyes. This man and I were already married in the spirit.

"So, how long are you going to make me wait before we put this destiny in motion."

I smiled a mischievous grin and said. "Don't make me get dressed right now."

"No, don't you play with me woman."

"Who said I'm playing?"

"You'd would marry me today?"

"I sure would."

"What about work, your career?"

"Grant, I love my career, but there's one Grant Carpenter," I said with conviction.

I was too tired to resist this destiny staring me in the face. Too tired to deny myself any longer a life of *real* joy. Too tired to risk this man disappearing from my life again.

As I looked at him, the back of my heart kicked me. Truly, for the first time I witnessed in his eyes what I know has always been in his. I didn't just see myself—I saw God in that man's eyes. A sincere recognition of unconditional love. I couldn't help but say, 'Hi God' like I'd done all those years ago by the barn.

At that moment something happened between us that moved us both to tears. This was it—all the suffering and pain was for this moment, this very moment that couldn't have happened until it's appointed time. Grant kissed me passionately again—not the way you might think. His passion is in his touch, his hand on my face that could be his own. The way his forehead cements to mine, his nose grazing mine and his mouth breathing air into mine forcing my head to fall backwards into his other hand. His tongue was absent from my mouth, yet I felt fulfilled with all we can share until our time in our undefiled marriage bed.

"I love you so much, Malena Dawson and I'd marry you today in a heartbeat, but I think we should be fair to our family."

"You're right. We've waited this long, let's do it right. We can do it next year."

Grant's eyes bucked, "Next year! Woman, you've got thirty days," he said, pulling me in closer to him, "I said we needed to be fair, not crazy."

"I smiled, laughed and agreed with him. I'm getting married in thirty days, on my *twenty-eighth* birthday, which is the twenty-eighth day of June to my gift from God.

Grant and Malena Carpenter At Last

I just wanted to let you know, these are not slave narratives; because this is not the day of slavery, or is it? You see I had a slave mentality because I wouldn't accept my freedom, so the master of emotions had me out in the fields in chains, tending to bad soil. I knew what love was, witnessed it with my very own eyes, not only with my parents, but Mrs. Mable, Pastor Simms and others. Knowing not everyone gets the chance to see that as a child.

Grant and I were fortunate that we both had the foundation of love. It's that love that I cried to so often that allowed me to talk to my Father in heaven, my grandparents and to you-the readers, our future children, grandchildren and anyone who dares to questions if Adam truly has a missing rib. I'm not sure what they will call our letters in the year 3000, but we hope our love is a testimony to help set you free to embrace life. A life that's not rooted in another person, but by grace and mercy you can share with someone else.

So forgive us if we didn't spend time talking about our looks, the clothes we wear, the cars we drive or the furnishing in our homes. We wanted to make sure that your eyes stayed fixed

128

on the decorator and carpenter of all things-God. And to see that love comes through His eyes first and foremost and once you receive it you can decorate love anyway you want to. I have to tell you, it's so great to finally have it feel so right. I never knew what making love was all about until Grant. Yes, he remained pure until our wedding night, but he's the most experienced lover I've ever known. He doesn't please my flesh, he pleases my spirit which is connected to his and honey let me tell you, it washed away every crooked dent in my past.

The kind of loving he gives me is not about physical acrobats…he enters from a level too deep to explain to you. When we're together in spirit, it's a fulfillment, a demanding secret that we have the privilege of experiencing together.

So again, all the hurt was worth the wait to get it RIGHT! And you know what, Grant has changed into an even better man. We both have, both evolving together.

I used to believe that I loved Grant because he made me feel so good, but I love him because he is good. If I had to use a word to describe our wedding, I'd say sacred. It was a very small gathering of twenty-five people consisting mostly of family. We wanted true witnesses surrounding us on such a glorious day. For a wedding gift, Grant gave me a sacred gift to pass onto our daughter on her wedding day-LOVE! I gave him a river of tears, at least that's what happened when he realized that I was taking his last name. I had no idea that he'd be moved in such a way. He was concerned because I had already established myself as Malena Dawson in the television industry. He had a point and I considered it for less than a second. The name Dawson had done all it could do for me-I knew that.

Like Momma said so many years ago, no one can take your memories. With all that I endured, it was like a road to Damascus experience and it was time for a new name, a new beginning. Besides, to keep my old name was to please the viewers and if God had blessed me with the name Dawson, how surely would he bless me by honoring his son and his created union. Grant and I are one in all ways, spirit, heart and name. Of course you know many (especially Pam) disagree with it and

I DON'T care about all that now. Grant is worth it, he's still kind, generous, loving, romantic and everything that he was before, even now ten years later.

In case you're wondering, changing my last name had an impact on my career, my talk show skyrocketed in the ratings and is now syndicated nationally. Daddy used to say God honors faithfulness to his earthly unions. It is the greatest honor in the world to be a servant of Jesus, to spread his gospel to others. According to the demographics, my show reaches the younger audiences. We receive letters from high school and college students, girls and boys who have given their life to Christ. Grant says that's why God called me so early to reach his kids, pull his kids back into the fold and help bring them back to the throne.

I just listen. That man has a connection with the Lord that is amazing at times. Things haven't always been smooth, but obstacles seem sweet when we overcome evil for good, so we never complain-just continue to give praise and thanks to the Lord. I have a co-host occasionally, none other than my delectable husband, who for my thirty-third birthday bought the station. He is now the C.E.O. of Anchor Broadcasting. You shouldn't be surprised that he's accumulated that kind of wealth. Remember his steps were always ordered by the Lord (truly ordered) and that lead him into everything. Some kill, lie and steal to get here and his came from listening, asking, and oh yeah, BELIEVING, in faith.

He still says his faith is like a blind man--you don't worry about bumping into a wall if you can't see it. So when he tells me to do something, I do it and I now live my life that same way in faith. By the way. I'm pregnant with our first child. Grant says it's going to be a girl and he wants to name her GIA (God Is Able). He's still the one and only lover of my heart playing second to the lover of my soul-Jesus Christ.

Okay, I have to go now. Grant just looked at me with those eyes and mouthed, "Pineapple" and I still can't deny him his sweet meat (minus the hard shell) now that I'm Mrs. Grant Carpenter. Forgive my blushing but I can't help myself when his eyes are calling me to him. But, we'll catch back up with you in thirty years to let you know how we're doing. Grant says in our eighties we'll still be as sweet as we are today-I trust that, I trust him, more importantly-WE trust in the Lord. So for now I thank you for sharing in the testimony of me and Grant, Grant and I.

Be sure to read the second chronicle of

The Cradle Robbers
Bloom

by
Linda Dominique Grosvenor

About the author

Tanya Marie Lewis is a writer based in Biloxi, Mississippi. She is founder and president of Out of Egypt Publishing, a small publishing company dedicated to enforcing/inspiring a positive change in ones life. She is an author, poet, and songwriter with a background in advertising and public relations. She is busy at work on her third Christian fiction novel.